The Zillah
REBELLION

**Books are to be returned on or before
the last date below.**

The Zillah REBELLION

HELEN DUNMORE

SCHOLASTIC
PRESS

Scholastic Children's Books,
Commonwealth House, 1-19 New Oxford Street,
London, WC1A 1NU, UK
a division of Scholastic Ltd
London ~ New York ~ Toronto ~ Sydney ~ Auckland
Mexico City ~ New Delhi ~ Hong Kong

First published in the UK by Scholastic Ltd, 2001

ISBN 0 439 99355 5

Typeset by DP Photosetting, Aylesbury, Bucks.
Printed at Mackays of Chatham Ltd.

10 9 8 7 6 5 4 3 2 1

Chapter One

It all began on a perfect summer day. Not a cloud in the sky, no worries, just the sun on my back and the sound of the sea.

Hmm. That's not *quite* true, is it? No worries at all? Not when Zillah had just told me that she was going up to see Granny Carne, and she wanted me to go with her?

I'd better tell you about Granny Carne first, or all this will sound completely crazy. I wouldn't get nervous about going to see a granny with pictures of her grandchildren on top of the TV, and a big tin of toffees for visitors. Granny Carne, however, is not like that at all. She's not related to Zillah at all, and she is the least cosy person in the whole of Cornwall. In fact she's a –

Better not say it. Better not even *think* it. Granny Carne looks as if she can hear your thoughts. She's very tall and she stands as straight as a tree so that she looks even taller. When she strides down the hill from her cottage with her coat blowing out behind her, she's like a bird of prey swooping on us.

Granny Carne has tough, outdoor skin and white hair. Sometimes her eyes are clear, piercing blue, and sometimes they're stormy, like the sea. I've seen her lots of times, but I've never talked to her. Once I met her in the lane. She was bending down by the hedge, picking leaves and putting them into a brown paper bag. I thought I might be able to get past without her seeing me, but she straightened up and her eyes swept over my face as if she could read it. I wanted to say hello, but nothing came out. Then she nodded, as if she'd found out all she wanted to know about me, and went back to picking the leaves. I wanted to run, but I wanted to stay, too. I wanted to say something to her, maybe ask her something. . .

"Katie? Katie? Hello?"

"What? Oh, sorry, Zill. I was thinking −"

"You will come with me, won't you, Katie?"

I rolled over on my beach towel so I could see her face. She looked fierce, determined, and very Zillah-ish.

"But Granny Carne doesn't even know me," I said. "She won't want me to come up to her cottage."

"Are you scared?"

"Scared?"

"You know. Of her."

"Course I'm not," I said, much too quickly.

"You are," said Zillah.

"Why should I be scared? She's just an old lady, isn't she?"

Zillah glanced round quickly, as if someone might overhear us.

"*I'm* scared, even though I've been up there loads of times," she said. "Even though I've known her all my life."

"Have you really been up there loads of times, Zillah? You never told me."

Zillah sat up, hugging her knees, and stared out to sea.

"I used to go with my Great-aunt Zillah, and then when she died I went on my own," she said. "You go up to Granny Carne's when you can't see your way clear ahead. When you want to know how things are going to be, or what you ought to do. You can ask her any questions you like."

"You mean she can tell you what's going to happen? She can really see into the future?"

"I don't know. People say she can. Some of the things she told me –" Zillah stopped suddenly, as if she'd said too much.

"What things?"

But Zillah wouldn't say. She shrugged and looked secretive.

"You'll have to see for yourself, Katie. You come with me. See what Granny Carne tells you."

It was a perfect summer day. There wasn't a cloud, or a breath of wind. There was nothing to be afraid of.

"She's not ... she's not a sort of ... *witch*, is she, Zillah?" The minute I'd said it I wished I hadn't. Saying things makes them real. And anyway, it sounded so stupid. Zillah would just laugh at me.

But Zillah didn't laugh. She frowned, and dug up a handful of sand, then let it trickle away through her fingers before answering. "There've always been witches round here," she said. "We're famous for them. But she's not a witch the way you mean."

"No spells? No cauldron?"

"And definitely no black cat either," said Zillah. "But Granny Carne knows things other people don't know. She can feel the future coming. She says that the past and present and future aren't really separate. They're all joined up, and if you know how to do it you can move from one to another and back again. She says time's like a long carpet, some of it rolled up, some of it spread out. All she has to do is unroll the part of the pattern that's been rolled up and hidden. But I don't know how she does it."

A prickle of shiver ran over my back and down my legs. It all sounded witchy enough to me.

"Does she tell you the bad things that are going to happen? I mean – if someone's going to die or something–"

"No," said Zillah quickly. "She won't tell you anything like that."

Zillah must have guessed that I was thinking of Dad. Dad had died in the middle of an ordinary Saturday morning more than a year ago. No one had known the accident was going to happen. I remember someone at the funeral saying, "*It came out of a clear blue sky.*"

"But – if she did – maybe people could avoid the bad thing that was going to happen to them –"

I thought about my dad fixing up the ladder Mr Riordan had lent him. Doing the catches up wrong, and hoping they were right. Starting to climb up the tall ladder into our lilac tree –

What if Dad had been to see Granny Carne? She might have been able to give him a warning – stop him from doing it – tell him to keep away from ladders –

But Dad could never have met Granny Carne. He'd never even been to Cornwall. If Dad was still alive we would still be living in London. I'd never have come to live in Cornwall. I'd never even have met Zillah – we wouldn't be talking about Granny Carne now...

It was running round and round in circles inside my head. I was beginning to feel dizzy.

"Katie?" Zillah was looking at me anxiously. "Are you all right?"

"I think she ought to tell people, if it could help them. Suppose she knew that someone was going on an aeroplane that was going to crash, and she didn't warn them."

"I don't think it works like that. Granny Carne says she can see the pattern, but she can't change it. She can unroll the carpet but she can't weave it differently. She never told my Great-aunt Zillah that she was going to get ill and die."

Zillah's great-aunt died nearly three years ago now. It was before I came to Cornwall, so I never knew her. But I feel as if I do, because of the way Zillah talks about her. Her great-aunt looked after Zillah all the time when she was little, while her parents worked on the farm. Zillah really loved her great-aunt...

"D'you want half this KitKat?" Zillah asked.

"Mmm, thanks –"

I always eat my chocolate bars straight away, but Zillah can keep hers for ages. Sometimes she even forgets about them, which I would never do in a million years. Once, when I was looking for my trainers, I found a whole Mars bar which had fallen down the side of her bed. *Zillah hadn't even bothered to look for it.*

"You don't have to come with me, Katie. I'll go on my own if you don't want to," said Zillah.

"I do want to, in a way. It's just that I've never talked to a witch."

"Everyone round here goes to Granny Carne. They keep quiet about it, but they all go. When they've got a question about the future, it doesn't matter what it is, they go up to Granny Carne's. She can't always help them, though. There are some people she can't help at all."

A picture floated into my mind. I saw Susie Buryan from our class, with her bouncy curls and her neat Guide's uniform, plodding up the path to find out about her future.

"Does Susie Buryan go?" I asked.

"You're joking. Anyway, she's too young. You have to be about sixteen before Granny Carne'll see you."

"But she sees *you*."

"That's because my Great-aunt Zillah was friends with Granny Carne. I always went along. She won't mind you coming either, because you're my friend. But Susie Buryan most definitely isn't. Mind, I've seen Susie's mum go up there."

Another picture replaced the picture of Susie in my mind.

Mrs Buryan, big and square and sensible in her waterproofs, jolting her Land Rover up the steep track to Granny Carne's cottage to have her fortune told.

"She doesn't, does she, Zillah? She looks much too – I don't know – too *practical*."

Zillah laughed. "Loads of people aren't as practical after dark as they are in the daytime." She brushed the sand off her legs. "You going to swim again?" she asked.

The sea was blue, but it was early in the year and the water hadn't warmed up yet. In fact, it was completely freezing. You had to plunge straight in because you would never, never manage it if you went in slowly. It was so cold you couldn't even scream. But if you swam really hard, kicking and thrashing and gasping, it began to feel as if you weren't going to die. And then suddenly it was wonderful.

"OK," I said.

We swam a little way out, but not too far. The sea's not tame round here. It's wild and fierce, and there are currents even on the calmest day. Zillah's taught me that. She says you've got to treat the sea right, if you want it to treat you right. You've got to show it respect.

I trod water, kicking hard to keep warm. Zillah dived down, deep into the purple and turquoise water. Down, down, down... I watched her shadow under the surface, twisting as she swam. Or was it Zillah? It didn't look like her any more. It looked like a seal, sleek and graceful, cutting through the water.

There are plenty of seals around here. But where was Zillah? She'd been down a long time – too long –

Just as I began to panic, Zillah's wet head shot up from the water. She shook her hair out of her eyes, and swam up close to me.

"Listen, Katie. Don't ever call her a witch. People don't like that. Just say we're going up to Granny Carne's if anyone asks you." She said it very quietly, almost in a whisper, as if someone might hear. But we were completely alone. There was only the empty, sparkling water, a few seagulls, and Zillah, and me.

Chapter Two

That was yesterday. It's not beach weather today. A thick white mist has come rolling in from the sea, and everything's hidden. I'm lying on my bed with the duvet curled around me, because it's cold with the mist and the damp clinging to everything. The foghorn down the coast is lowing like a cow that's lost her calf.

I know about things that like that now: cows, and foghorns. A year ago, when we were still living in London, I wouldn't have known why the foghorn booms like that. It's to warn the ships about the sharp black needles of rock that run out from the cliffs around here, underwater. If a ship runs on to those rocks, it won't have a chance. It'll be ripped open, and then it will sink.

There have been hundreds of wrecks all down this coast. Mum showed me a Wrecks Map in the museum, which was covered with dots where ships had gone down. The name of each lost ship was written in beautiful, tiny handwriting, next to each dot.

"All those lives lost," Mum said. "All those stories no one knows any more."

I glanced at her quickly, but her face wasn't sad. Although it's more than a year since Dad died, sometimes it doesn't seem like a minute.

"Think of the people waiting for them to come home," said Mum. "All those wives and children."

But I didn't want to think of them. I wandered away from the map, and after a while Mum stopped looking at it, too.

Mum's a painter. She used to illustrate children's books as well, but since we've lived here she's painted the sea, and the cliffs and rocks, and the weather coming. The weather comes in fast here, and it changes all the time. Mum paints the sea when it's flat and glittery, and she paints it when it's so wild that slabs of foam break off and slap on to the rocks. On days like that you can taste salt in the wind.

People from cities come here and they want to buy some of the wildness. But they can't do that, so sometimes they buy one of Mum's paintings instead. Mum has sold five paintings, eight charcoal drawings and four little collages since we came here last October. I keep the accounts for her, because I'm good with money. She has to pay Robert's commission (he's the gallery owner, and he sells Mum's paintings for her). Robert's commission is a third of the selling price. So...

Mum's work has sold for £4,500 altogether, Robert has taken a third of that, which is £1,500, and that means we've had £3,000. We're doing really well.

Robert thinks Mum's prices could go higher now. I think Robert's commission could go lower, but Mum won't let me say anything about that. She says it's very fair, because most dealers charge fifty per cent. Fifty per cent! Can you imagine that? Mum sweats for weeks over a painting, then someone else gets *half the money* just for putting it in his shop and selling it. A third is bad enough. Robert can't even paint.

But Mum's grateful to Robert.

"Katie, Robert's been very good to me. If it hadn't been for his support, I'd never have sold any paintings at all."

Hmmm. Whenever I'm in St Ives I go into Robert's shop. There are always people looking at Mum's work, and asking about it. More people than there are looking at anyone else's. And Mum's work always sells quickly. Is Robert doing Mum a favour, or is Mum doing Robert a favour? But I don't say anything. I'm waiting for the right moment. Mum isn't so good with money, but I am. I'm planning to become her manager.

I don't like fog. It's the only weather I don't like. It makes me feel ... uneasy. As if something's about to happen, and not something good.

And it's today that me and Zillah are going to see the –

I mean, it's today that me and Zillah are going up to Granny Carne's.

If Granny Carne really can see into the future, there are loads of things I want to know. For instance:

1) Why has Zillah been in a bad mood for the past two weeks, even though she's trying to pretend she isn't? And has it got anything to do with the two men we saw measuring in their high field when we got off the school bus the Thursday before last? When Zillah saw them she stopped still and her mouth clamped together. She looked as if she'd like to kill someone. I asked her what the matter was – "Nothing, Katie. I'm fine," she said, in a voice like a shut door.

"I'll phone you later," I said when we got to the farm gate where Zillah turns off the lane. I love saying that. *I'll phone you later*. Only people who have lived without a telephone for seven months can understand how wonderful it is when your mum sells a painting and says, "Katie, do you know, I think we can afford to have a phone put in now."

2) (*More things I want to know about the future*.)

We've been here since October. We've got the cottage for a year. It's June now, so that means we might be leaving in four months' time. But *are* we going to leave? Will we go back to London, to our old house? Is our Cornwall life going to come to an end, just like that?

And do I want to go back to London? I thought I did. All my friends were there. Our house was there. I was born there. But now it's not so easy. The friends I've made here in Cornwall get more important every day, and my London friends get –

Not less important. But they're not my everyday friends now. They're not the friends I phone about homework, or what we're going to do on Saturday.

3) (*Still thinking of what to ask Granny Carne...*) Why is Mr T, our favourite computer-crazy head teacher, in an even worse mood than Zillah?

And what's wrong with Mrs T? Yesterday, when I came out into the playground at break, I saw her on the other side of the playground wall. She was rushing around her garden trying to catch the horrible new hens Mr Trevelyan bought for her, to replace the old ones which were eaten by a fox. (Mrs T was grateful to the fox, but Mr T didn't understand that, because he thinks that organic, free-range hens ordered from the internet are the best present anyone could possibly hope for.)

The hens are always escaping. As I watched, one of them jumped on to the pram handle and then flopped inside the pram, squawking and showering up feathers. I called to Mrs T, "Shall I come and help you catch them?"

I'm good at catching hens now. But Mrs T didn't even turn round.

"No thanks, Katie," she called in a voice that sounded strange, almost as if she was. . .

The hens are always getting out of their run, and Mrs T hates it. They peck the baby's legs when he's trying to learn to walk. But surely the hens wouldn't make Mrs T cry. . .

But I don't know if I can ask the witch – I mean, Granny Carne – about all this. These aren't real proper questions about the future, are they? Zillah says you can ask her anything you like, but I'm not sure. I don't want to sound stupid.

Besides, no matter what Zillah says, I'm still a bit –

Not frightened. No. I'm writing this on Mum's computer, and I've just looked up the word "frightened" in the thesaurus.

Scared, aghast, apprehensive, terrified, fearful, nervous, paranoid, disconcerted, afraid. . .

I don't think I'm any of these.

Zillah's coming at half-past two. It's about an hour's walk, she says. So at half-past three, I might know my future. I always feel sorry for sports stars when TV interviewers shove a mike in front of them before a big match, and ask them how they feel.

"So how do you feel at this moment, Katie, now that the big event is only an hour away?"

"Oh, I don't know. Just a little bit *disconcerted*, maybe."

Chapter Three

8.30 pm

Zillah has just left. It's a beautiful golden evening, and Mum's gone for a walk along the cliff path. She asked me to come with her, but I said I was tired.

But I'm so not-tired that I don't think I'll be able to sleep tonight. I'm not even going to try. So much has happened today, and I need to be on my own to try and work out what it all means.

Zillah was late. It was nearly three o'clock by the time she arrived, and by then I was very disconcerted indeed. And *aghast, paranoid, apprehensive, fearful* and quite a lot of other things as well. I was leaning out of my bedroom window to look for Zillah, and so I saw her before she saw me. She was red in the face, out of breath, and she looked furious. What was going on? And would she tell me about it at last?

She wouldn't.

"Sorry I'm late."

"That's OK."

"We'd better run. Granny Carne doesn't like it if people keep her waiting."

"But Zillah, it's nearly two miles!"

"Well, we can run part of it, can't we?" snapped Zillah.

"I can if you can," I snapped back.

The mist was still heavy. It was like running into a white tunnel that opened up just a few metres ahead, and then closed again behind us. Our footsteps thudded and stones rattled away from our trainers. We had to go up the lane, turn right, zig-zag behind the church and then take the footpath that runs up the fields to the bottom of the hill. Granny Carne's cottage was high up, Zillah had told me. It was in among the furze and boulders, tucked away so you couldn't see it until you were almost there.

"It's this way," panted Zillah, when we got to the top of the fields.

"Let's stop for a minute."

As soon as we stood still, the mist seemed to push in all around us, swallowing us. I couldn't even see the hedges. The foghorn boomed again, but I couldn't tell where it was coming from. The sea was invisible.

"We'd better go on," I said reluctantly.

"OK." Neither of us felt like running any more. Zillah picked a foxglove head as we scrambled up the steep path. She tore off the bells one by one, and her face was more closed and miserable than ever. I wished she'd tell me what was the matter. But I wasn't going to ask. I hate the kind of friends who are always trying to find out what you're thinking.

Suddenly, as if she'd made up her mind about something, Zillah threw away the foxglove stalk.

"Mum and Dad are so stupid," she said. Her voice was tight with anger. "You're lucky, Katie. Your mum listens to you. She's like a friend. My mum says to me, '*You don't understand, Zillah. You're too young. We have to think about the future.*'"

"What does she mean?"

"She means that she and Dad are the only ones who can make decisions. I bet it's not like that in your house, is it? Your mum talks things over with you."

"Yes. But Zillah—"

"What?"

"It might be because there's only me and Mum in my family."

"No. Your mum would be like that anyway."

"What do your parents mean, when they say they have to think about the future?"

"They mean they've got an insane, ridiculous plan, and they were trying to fix it all up without even telling me. They've already had surveyors round, measuring up our fields. They've even had builders in giving estimates."

"They're not going to build houses on your fields!"

"No, who'd want to live up here? There aren't any jobs or shops or anything. They're going to build a caravan park with showers and toilets and a café. Mum and Dad think they're going to make loads of money. They're planning to call it 'Seaside Farm'. What a lie."

"Well, it *is* quite near the sea…"

"Seaside means a nice sandy beach with an ice-cream van on it. What we're near is a huge cliff which all the holiday people's little kids will fall down. You know what it's like climbing down to our beach, Katie, and it's even worse getting to the cove. It's dangerous, unless you know the path like we do. There's no beach at high tide, anyway, just rocks. So calling it 'Seaside Farm' is just a *misrepresentation of the facts*."

Zillah reads more than anyone else I know. She knows about ten times more words than either of her parents, and never needs to consult the computer thesaurus at all.

"But how are your mum and dad going to afford to build a caravan park anyway? It'll cost loads to build shower-blocks and a café."

Zillah's parents haven't got any money. They won't touch a penny of the thirty-thousand pounds Zillah got from selling the diamond ring her

Great-aunt Zillah left to her. Zillah's begged her parents to share the money, but they are *so obstinate.*

"*That money's all for your future, girl. It belongs rightly to you.*" I've heard her dad say that, and then he and Janice (Zillah's mum) look at each other in a satisfied way which makes Zillah feel like throwing things at them.

Times are hard for farmers round here. Zillah's mum and dad work all the hours God sends. (That's what my mum says when she sees Janice humping chicken-feed at nine o'clock at night, or Geoff up on the roof, patching it for the hundredth time where a gale's taken the tiles off.) But they still don't make any money, and the bills still keep coming in. And Zillah's got thirty-thousand pounds lying in the bank! Zillah's right. Her parents are crazy.

"They're going to borrow the money," said Zillah. "These two developers came round and convinced them that they're going to make loads of money once the caravan park gets going, and they'll be able to pay the loans back. My parents are going to borrow all the money from the developers. Shift & Partner, they're called."

"How much are they borrowing?"

"They won't tell me, so it must be shed-loads. Dad keeps saying, '*This is the way ahead, Zill. We've got to look to the future.*'"

"Well, maybe it will work—"

21

"No, it won't. Not with Mum and Dad. They're not money people, they're farmers. They don't know anything about running a caravan park. They believe everything the developers tell them, but I don't. Shift & Partner are slime-balls. They keep a straight face but they're laughing at us inside. And that's not even the worst part of it."

"What's the worst part?"

Zillah's hands clenched on the stalk of another foxglove.

"I can't tell you. But I've got to stop them. That's why I'm going to see Granny Carne. She'll be able to tell me what to do, I know she will."

But when we knocked on Granny Carne's door, no one answered.

"D'you think she's gone out?"

"We're so late, maybe she thought we weren't coming."

I hoped Zillah couldn't tell how relieved I felt. The little grey cottage looked peaceful, tucked away in the ferns and furze. There were two big boulders in her garden, one balanced on top of the other. They looked as if they could fall at any moment, but I knew they'd probably been there for thousands of years. There are stones like that all round here. Zillah calls them *logans*.

"I'll knock once more," said Zillah.

The bang of the knocker echoed in the mist.

"Zillah! Look at the stone!"

"What?"

"It moved!"

Zillah stared. "No, it's not moving, Katie."

"It did move. I saw it. The top stone was rocking."

But now everything was quite still. The echo of the knocker died away. The huge, grey, granite stones looked as if they hadn't moved for a thousand years. And then the door sprang open, so suddenly that Zillah almost fell into the cottage. Granny Carne was standing there.

"Hello, Zillah. And this is your friend, Katie."

It wasn't a question. Zillah must have told her my name.

"Hello," I said squeakily.

Granny Carne gave me the look she'd given me before in the lane, reading my face, reading me. Then she nodded, and said, "Come on in, both of you."

The cottage was quite different from what I'd expected. It wasn't like any granny's home I'd ever visited. The cottage was so small that the whole downstairs was a single room, with the kitchen part at one end and a sofa at the other. The walls were white, and the chairs and sofa were covered in brilliant green, exactly the colour of new leaves.

There were no ornaments, and no photos. More importantly, there was no black cat, no cauldron, no spells, no bunches of herbs hanging from the ceiling, and no broomstick behind the door.

Something else was missing, too. I looked round again, and then I spotted what it was. There was no TV, no radio, no hi-fi. I looked up at the ceiling. There were no light bulbs either.

"The electric doesn't come up here," said Granny Carne. "And I can't be bothered with a generator."

"Can Katie see your spring?" asked Zillah.

"Later she can. Are you thirsty after your walk?" She crossed to the sink and poured water into two tall glasses, and handed them to Zillah and me. Zillah drank straight away, but I hesitated. Granny Carne watched me. She wasn't smiling, but her eyes were amused. I was sure that she knew the stories that were going through my head, about people who'd taken food and drink from witches, and fallen under their spell. My face was going red. To hide it, I lifted the glass, and the water touched my lips.

I drank. Once I'd started I realized how thirsty I was, and I didn't stop until I'd finished the glass.

"That's my spring water," said Granny Carne. "I pump it through to the tank. Zillah will show you later. Now, we'll sit down."

We sat at the kitchen table, Zillah and me on one side, Granny Carne facing us on the other.

"Who's going to begin?" she asked.

"I will," said Zillah.

"Will Katie stay to hear it?"

Zillah gave me the first real smile I'd seen on her face for two weeks.

"Katie's my friend," she said.

It all looked so simple. Zillah changed places with me so that she was sitting directly opposite Granny Carne. Granny Carne stretched out her hand over the table, and Zillah stretched out hers and laid it on Granny Carne's, palm up. Granny Carne said nothing at first. She glanced at Zillah's face, then down at her hand, then up at her face again. Then she spread Zillah's hand flat and looked at it closely, for a long time. No one said anything. Nothing moved. After a few minutes Granny Carne nodded, as if to say, "That's enough," and Zillah laid her hands back in her lap.

Granny Carne closed her eyes and began to speak. Her voice was still the same everyday voice as the one she'd used when she asked us if we'd like a drink of water. But her face had changed and it was harsh and strong. She looked like one of the granite stones in her garden. She looked as if she'd been staring into Zillah's future for a thousand years.

"You've come up here because you see changes ahead of you. You don't know your way ahead."

Oh yes she does, I thought. She wants to stop her mum and dad building a caravan park.

"You don't know what you can do," said Granny Carne. "You don't know where your power lies."

Zillah was staring intently into Granny Carne's face. Granny Carne's eyes were still shut, as if she was listening to something we couldn't hear. Was she moving? Was she rocking, just a little, to and fro, like her stones?

"The sea'll look after you," said Granny Carne suddenly.

Zillah leaned forward, her eyes fixed on Granny Carne.

"The sea? What do you mean?" Her voice was sharp. This wasn't what we'd come for.

There was a long silence. "I've got nothing more for you, Zillah," said Granny Carne, and she opened her eyes. Zillah stared as if she couldn't believe it.

"I've nothing more for you, Zillah," repeated Granny Carne.

Slowly, reluctantly, Zillah got up, and we changed places so that now I was sitting opposite Granny Carne. I stretched out my hand, as Zillah had done, palm upward. Granny Carne ran her hand lightly over mine so that my fingers were completely flat.

"Look at me, Katie," she said.

But I didn't want to look. Suddenly I didn't want to know anything at all about the future, my own or

Zillah's or anyone else's. I wanted to stay here, in the present. I wanted to keep the door to the future tightly shut.

"You've done well," said Granny Carne.

I stared at her. That wasn't what I'd expected her to say at all. Her eyes were a clear, sharp, everyday blue. There was nothing strange or mysterious in them.

"I'm not going to open that door, unless you want me to," said Granny Carne.

"No, I don't – I don't want –"

"That's all right. You're doing well here with us, Katie. This is the place for you."

I took a deep breath. Suddenly I felt warm and relaxed, as if I was sitting in the sun. She was right. I wanted to be here. It was the right place for me. I didn't want to go back to London. Now Granny Carne had said it, I realized that I'd known it for weeks. Months, maybe.

I didn't want to get up from the table. I wanted to go on sitting there, with Granny Carne telling me how well I'd done, and that I belonged here now. Just for this moment there was no need to worry about the past, or the future. The present was all that mattered.

"You come and see my spring," said Granny Carne. Zillah and I got up stiffly, as if we'd been sitting there for a long time. But it was only minutes.

We followed Granny Carne to a little door at the back of the cottage, and squeezed through it, ducking our heads.

We were out in the sun. The mist had disappeared. A steep hill rose in front of us like a green wall, covered in moss and bracken, and there was a bubbling, chuckling sound of water.

"It's this way," said Zillah.

Cut into the side of the hill there was a stone trough, full of bright, clear water. Tiny plants and flowers grew around the edge of it, and there was a hole in its stone base. Granny Carne's spring was swelling up inside the trough like an underwater fountain.

"This is where my spring rises," said Granny Carne.

"Did you make the trough?" I asked.

"No, he's been here a long time. Before my great-grandma's time, when she was a girl."

I tried to work out in my head how long that was. Granny Carne must be really old. More than seventy, maybe even eighty. Her great-grandma could have been born nearly two hundred years ago. . .

"And that old spring's been giving us good water all those years," said Granny Carne. She showed us where she'd run piping from the trough, to a tank which served the cottage.

"It fills up my tank, so I'm never without. This spring never fails, even in drought."

I stared into the trough. The water was so clear you could see the stone patterns cut into the sides of the trough. I wanted to touch them.

"You touch if you like," said Granny Carne.

I put my hand into the cold, clear water, and felt the patterns. They were strong and deep. I wondered who had cut them there, hundreds of years before.

"That's old stone, that is," said Granny Carne. "When they made the trough they would have taken old stone for it. Those carvings weren't made in our history."

I lifted my hand out of the water. Drops ran off it on to the mossy ground. I wished our water bubbled into a trough like this, out of the side of a hill, cold and sweet.

"So you'll come back and see me one of these days," said Granny Carne. I nodded. Zillah was staring dreamily into the water, a half-smile on her face, as if she'd forgotten all her worries.

"You've drunk my water," said Granny Carne. "You'll be back."

Chapter Four

Mum's just got back from her walk. Although it's late, it's still not quite dark. Mum says that's because we're so far west, and these are the longest days of the summer. If I turn off my light, and look out of my bedroom window, I can see the stars coming out one by one.

Mum was gone for ages. She forgets the time when she's out on the cliffs, sketching. I don't worry about her really, but I don't like her being out too late, so I thought I'd walk down to meet her. And then maybe all the stuff that had happened at Granny Carne's would stop going round and round in my head.

I went down across the fields, where nothing grows any more except brambles, heather, furze and bracken. You can tell that people used to farm these fields all the way down to the cliffs once, because there are stone walls built around them. It must have taken a long time to build all those walls, so carefully. Zillah's dad told me once that the walls were put there to keep the salt wind off the crops, and stop the topsoil from blowing away. And if there were cows in the fields, they could shelter. Cows always find a place out of the wind if they can.

The dew was coming down and the long grass was wet. I love the smell of summer evenings around here. No petrol fumes, no tired, dirty air. There's a smell of grass, and warm earth, and the sea...

"And cowpats," Zillah always says. "Don't forget the cowpats, Katie."

I saw Mum away in the distance, wandering along with her sketchbook under her arm. I waved, and she waved back.

"What time is it, Katie?" she asked when I came up to her.

"Um – about ten o'clock," I said.

"School tomorrow. We'd better get back."

But I could tell she didn't want to, any more than I did. She looked around and sighed.

"I climbed down to the cove," she said. "You know those two seals that sometimes come in? They were there this evening. I'm sure they were in the middle of a game, and I interrupted them."

"What were they doing?"

"Diving deep down and then shooting up as close as they could to each other. Do you know, Katie, if

I'd been in the water I'm sure they'd have let me join in. You know how curious they are. When they saw me they swam up really close. I think they wanted some fish, but I hadn't got anything for them. Have you and Zillah been feeding them?"

"We do sometimes, if we've caught enough mackerel."

Zillah showed me how to do it. You throw the fish up high and the seals dive just as it comes down and then they catch it as it falls through the water. The mackerel slides headlong into the seal's mouth, like a letter going into a postbox. They never miss.

"I never thought I'd live somewhere I could go out for a walk in the evening and talk to seals," said Mum.

"Did you really talk to them, Mum?"

"Oh yes, I told them all sorts of things. I'm sure they understand."

"That's what Zillah says. She talks to them as well."

I didn't tell Mum that sometimes we swim with the seals. We aren't really supposed to swim at high tide, which is the time when the seals come right in. There's no beach then, and you have to jump off the rocks and then scramble back up. Mum thinks it's dangerous, because a wave might throw us against the rocks, but we're very careful. We never swim when it's rough. The seals don't come close while we're swimming, but we can see their wet, black heads and their whiskers and their big, curious eyes. Mum's right, they do look as if they understand everything you say.

I wish they'd come closer. Zillah says they will one day, later on in the summer, when they're more used to us.

Mum sighed happily. "It's so peaceful here," she said, looking around. I looked around too. I looked up towards our cottage, and beyond it, to the farm where Zillah lived. Those were the fields the surveyors had been measuring. That was where the developers were planning the caravan park, and the shower-block and toilet-block, and the car park. Suddenly I had a picture of what it would be like. Cars everywhere. Caravans. Music from the café. Radios playing and kids yelling and mobile phones ringing. It certainly wouldn't be peaceful any more. What about the seals? Would the noise scare them off so they wouldn't come into the cove any more?

"Mum..." I began cautiously. "Can anyone build what they like in the country?"

"What?"

"I mean, if you've got a field, can you just build what you like in it?"

"Oh no, I don't think so," said Mum. "You've got to have planning permission to build houses."

"What about – what about temporary houses?"

"Temporary houses? I don't know what you mean, Katie."

"Well, like ... caravans."

Mum frowned. "Now you ask me, I'm not sure. You do see a lot of caravan sites all over the place. I suppose if it's your land, there's no reason why not."

"So you could put a caravan park anywhere?"

"Not right by our cottage, Katie," said Mum, laughing. "Is that your latest get-rich-quick scheme? The land's not ours, it belongs to Geoff and Janice."

"I know it does," I said. "I'm not stupid. But *they* could build one, if they wanted—"

"Oh no, that'll never happen," said Mum confidently. "Janice and Geoff aren't interested. They run a working farm. They're partners in it, and that's how they like it. Janice has told me that lots of times. That's why she doesn't do bed and breakfast, or anything like that. She says it's not worth the time it takes up. Just think about it, Katie. They could easily rent out our cottage as a holiday cottage, but they don't. So you can tell they're not interested."

They could easily rent out our cottage as a holiday cottage... I stared at Mum, then quickly looked away so she wouldn't guess what I was thinking. Zillah's words leaped into my mind. *"And that's not even the worst part of it... I can't tell you... But I'm going to stop them."*

34

Was our cottage part of Geoff and Janice's *Seaside Farm* plans? Was that why Zillah was so angry?

"Mum . . . you know you said Janice was letting us live in the cottage for a year from last October? Can we stay on after this October, if we want to?"

"Oh yes, I'm sure we can. I can pay Janice a proper rent, now that my work's going so well, and I'm selling paintings. I'm sure there won't be a problem. After all, Katie, Janice is one of my oldest friends."

Poor Mum. She looked so happy and relaxed, strolling along in the the summer dusk. For the first time in our lives I felt as if I was the adult, and she was the child. There were things which I knew, and Mum didn't.

And I was determined to keep it that way. I couldn't bear Mum to go back to the way she'd been in the months after Dad died. I didn't want to wake up in the dead of night and hear her moving about downstairs because she couldn't sleep, couldn't paint, couldn't do anything except think over and over about what had happened to Dad.

"Come on, Mum, it's really late. I should be in bed."

Granny Carne says this is the place for me. She's right. No one is going to change that. I won't let them.

It's strange, isn't it? I'm starting to sound like Zillah. She's always been the fierce, determined one, not me. But maybe I'm changing. . .

Chapter Five

I've just got home from school.

I can't believe it. I just can't believe what Mrs T told me today.

But she says everyone will know tomorrow. Mr T's going to tell us in Assembly.

I can't believe it, I –

Katie, no one is ever going to know what you're talking about if you start the story in the middle. Dad used to say that.

So I'll begin at the beginning.

It was ten o'clock in the morning, half an hour to go before break. Mr T sent me out to the playground to check on our rainfall gauges and record the results. It's part of a project on climate change that we're doing, in partnership with our internet-linked twin school in Yakutsk. This is the kind of project that Mr T loves. As I've already mentioned, he is obsessed with being in touch with the whole world through computers.

I was about to check the first gauge when I heard Mrs T's voice. "Katie! Katie!"

She was calling quietly, as if she didn't want anyone else to hear. All our classroom windows were wide open because of the hot weather.

"Katie!"

I left the gauge and went over to the wall where she was standing. Their garden backs on to the playground, and usually all the little Ts are running round, chasing hens and giving their puppy a ride in the pushchair and so on. Mr and Mrs T have got three little kids who aren't old enough to go to school yet. But today the garden was empty and quiet.

"Where are they?" I asked.

"My mother's got them. She's come down like an absolute angel of mercy and taken them off to St Ives for the day."

That's the way Mrs T talks. She has a Range-Rover voice but a tractor life. She's the first real grown-up friend I've ever had. I don't mean a grown-up who's nice to you: I mean a grown-up who's a friend. And then I noticed something else that was different, apart from the peace and quiet. Mrs T was wearing a black skirt, a white shirt and a black jacket. They were a bit loose on her, but they were still about a million times smarter than anything I'd ever seen her wearing. Usually she wears jeans with chocolate fingermarks on them, and T-shirts which the baby has rubbed biscuit all over.

"Why are you wearing those clothes? Are you going somewhere?"

"Oh dear, they do look a bit bizarre, don't they? They're my mother's. But I had to borrow them. I've got to look right."

"Right for what?"

Mrs T took a deep breath. "Katie, can you do something for me? Can you say to Mr T: 'Mrs T said to tell you that they've gone over to St Ives for the day.'"

"But – but you aren't going to sit on the beach dressed like that, are you?"

"No. But I don't want him to know where I'm really going until I get back."

"Oh."

"Because he might try and stop me –" She was talking to herself really, not to me. But what was she talking about? What was Mr T going to try and stop her from doing?

"I'm sorry, Katie," said Mrs T suddenly. "I shouldn't drag you into this without telling you what it's all about. You'll hear about it tomorrow anyway. Richard's decided to tell the whole school, because he's afraid it'll get on to the grapevine by the end of the week anyway."

"What will? What'll get on to the grapevine?" I was feeling really frightened now. Maybe someone was ill. Maybe Mr and Mrs T were going to get divorced and Mrs T was going to see a solicitor about it in Truro. Maybe—

"They're planning to close the school." Even with her tan, she was pale. "I'm going to talk to the Chair of the Education Committee."

"But – they can't –"

"No," said Mrs T grimly. "They can't. It's our school. It's sixty-eight children's school. It's your lives, and our lives. It's Richard's whole life."

"Close our school? But when?"

"At the end of this year. They'll do the reorganization over the summer, and all the pupils will be given places at the primary school closest to their homes. They say there aren't enough children coming in to make this school viable. They say they've done a feasibility study, and a population study, and they've looked into the economics. And so we've got to close. It doesn't matter that sixty-eight children are happy here."

The way Mrs T said "population study" and "economics", they sounded like swear words. I looked around the playground, at the bench where Top Group usually sat under the tree for quiet reading, at the painted hopscotch lines and the wooden toy train where the little ones played, at the wide-open classroom windows. I heard the hum of the school coming through the windows.

"But, Mrs T, it can't all stop, just like that."

"They think it can." Mrs T's face quivered for a moment, then she drew herself up straight and fierce. "I am *not* going to let it happen," she said. "Don't tell anyone except Zillah today, Katie. You'll all be told tomorrow. I'd better go. Oh God, those bloody, bloody hens are eating my lettuces again. . ." She dived towards the hens.

"Mrs T! Mind your clothes! You mustn't get feathers all over them."

Mrs T stopped as if I'd put the brakes on. "I'd *like* to get chicken feathers all over the Chair of the Education Committee, but I don't suppose he'd take me seriously. . . Katie, I've got to dash. Thank God you came out. I'd have exploded if I hadn't been able to talk to you. My mother is trying her best to be sympathetic, but I know she'd love it if the school closed. She thinks I'm absolutely *buried* in mud and chickens down here, and wouldn't it be marvellous to get me back into civilization again? Do you know, Katie, I never thought I'd say it, but when I think of civilization, I feel *quite fond* of these appalling hens."

A minute later she was gone and I was alone in the sunny playground. For a moment I couldn't remember what I was supposed to be doing. Oh yes, the rain-gauges. But there wouldn't be any rain in them anyway, because it had been fine all week.

"Make sure you *check* those gauges, Katie! It might have been raining at night. This is scientific investigation, not guesswork. Our friends in Yakutsk are relying on us." That was what Mr T had said. I knelt down and checked the first gauge. And there was rain in it, just a tiny bit. It must have rained in the night after all. I wrote it down carefully on my chart. I'd have to hurry. I'd been ages talking to Mrs T – and I mustn't forget to give Mr T her message: "*Mrs T says to tell you they've gone over to St Ives for the day.*"

It wasn't really a lie. Mrs T's mum and the children *had* gone to St Ives. I wasn't going to say that Mrs T had gone as well – but if Mr T wanted to think that she had –

"*...and so we've got to close... It doesn't matter that sixty-eight children are happy here ... population study ... economics...*"

They can't do it!

Chapter Six

"They can, though, can't they," said Zillah slowly. "They've got all the power."

"But it's our school."

"I know."

I hadn't told Zillah the news at school or on the school bus, in case someone else heard. I'd waited until the bus had driven off, leaving us alone at the top of the lane.

"We've got to think. Listen, Katie, come up to my house for a bit?"

"Yes, if I phone Mum to tell her."

Zillah's mum, Janice, was sitting at the kitchen table with lots of papers spread out in front of her. She jumped when she saw me.

"Katie! I didn't know you were coming." She didn't sound at all pleased to see me. Usually Janice asks me to tea if I come up to the farm after school, but not today. Flustered and embarrassed, she swept the papers together and hugged them to her. "I'll just – I'll just put these away –" And she hurried out of the kitchen. Zillah looked furious. "She's looking at those plans again."

No wonder Janice wasn't pleased to see me. I wasn't supposed to know anything about the caravan park.

"Maybe I should go..."

"No, don't go," said Zillah. "Let's go out to the orchard."

I phoned Mum, Zillah grabbed a handful of biscuits from the tin and we headed outside. The orchard is a tiny field with six stunted apple trees in it, where Janice's hens run. There's too much wind here for apple trees to grow properly. We lay down in the grass, and all the hens squawked off to the other end of the orchard, complaining about us. Zillah shared out the ginger snaps.

"Sorry about Mum," she said awkwardly.

"That's OK."

I kept wishing I'd seen those plans. Then I'd know for sure what was going to happen about our cottage. October wasn't far away. It seemed impossible that everything could change so quickly.

But I knew that it could. My whole life had changed in a day, when Dad died. And tomorrow morning Mr Trevelyan was going to announce to the whole school that it was going to be closed. Because there are only sixty-eight of us in our school, we only have two classes, Key Stage One and Key Stage Two.

Everybody would be there in the hall, with the little ones in a row at the front. I imagined the little ones staring up at Mr Trevelyan, playing with the velcro on their trainers and not understanding what he meant.

"Everything's changing! I hate it!" I didn't mean to say that. The words leaped out of my mouth before I knew they were there.

"Everything was changing anyway," said Zillah slowly. She picked up a hard, green baby apple that had fallen from the tree, and flicked it high into the sky. "For us, I mean. After all, we're leaving at the end of term. We'll be at secondary school in September."

I couldn't believe it. Zillah's been at our school since she was in Reception, years and years longer than me. How could she sound so calm? "Don't you care if the school closes?"

Zillah flicked another apple and we both watched it spin upwards. "Of course I do. But I've got to stop Mum and Dad first. That's more important. Once they start building that caravan park, everything's finished here."

Again, I wondered what Zillah knew that she couldn't tell me. If only I could see those plans...

"Zillah."

"Mmm?"

"I'm just going up to the house. I need the toilet."

"OK."

Zillah lay back and shut her eyes. I shut the orchard gate so the hens couldn't get out, and crossed the yard to the farmhouse door. My heart was beating hard. I was going to do something I'd never done before.

I paused at the back door, which led straight into the kitchen. It was slightly open. I could hear the radio, and then the clink of plates. Janice was in there, cooking. Zillah had told me earlier that her father had gone over to Penzance.

Bobby, the Treliskes' Labrador, came bounding round the side of the farmhouse. I knelt down to him and let him lick my hands.

"It's only me. Now, you be a good, quiet boy, and don't bark while I just fetch something from inside the house."

Bobby stared at me with his intelligent eyes. He knew I wasn't a burglar. He wasn't going to give the game away.

"Good boy, Bobby." Bobby wagged his tail, and I felt awful. Lying to human beings is bad enough, but somehow lying to animals is even worse. I walked softly round the side of the farmhouse until I reached what Janice called the parlour door. They hardly ever used it, but they only locked it at night. I turned the handle gently, gently...

I was in the hall, just by the stairs. Kitchen sounds floated down the passage. So Janice was still safely in there. The house smelled of baking. Janice is brilliant at cake-making, but unfortunately Zillah and Geoff don't really like cake, so she has to bake for WI sales. I trod lightly up the stairs. There was the bathroom door. If Janice came out, I was only going to the toilet. There, opposite, was Janice and Geoff's bedroom door.

The door creaked loudly as I opened it. The bedroom was unbelievably neat. It didn't look as if anyone slept there. Two narrow beds, a wardrobe, a dressing-table. No bedside tables, no lamps. No clutter. And no papers.

I was backing out of the door when I saw it. On the broad, low windowsill, nearly hidden by the curtain. A pile of papers, almost pushed into hiding. But she'd been in a hurry.

I stopped again, and listened. Nothing moved in the house. I crossed the boards, testing them to make sure they didn't creak. Those were the papers Janice had been reading in the kitchen, I was sure of it. A pile, but not a neat pile. She wouldn't notice if I touched them.

And now quick. I lifted one paper, then the next. Lists of figures, letters on headed paper. *Shift & Partner*. More figures.

And then I found them. Drawings. But not proper drawings which showed you how things would look. These were carefully scaled boxes on squared paper. But there were words too. *Treliske Farm*, that was one box. And down the lane, another little box. *Holiday Centre*. But it looked so familiar. Just down the lane, less than ten minutes' walk, or five minutes' run. One field, two field, three fields … I measured the distance with my fingers.

It was our cottage. Geoff and Janice and Shift & Partner were planning to turn our cottage into a Holiday Centre.

"*But it's not really your cottage, is it?*" said a cold little voice inside my head. "*It belongs to the Treliskes. You've got to be out of there in October.*" And then I heard Mum's voice, confident and relaxed, "*After all, Katie, Janice is one of my oldest friends.*"

I dropped the sheet of paper. Then, quickly and carefully, I remade the pile so that everything was back in order. I shut Janice and Geoff's bedroom door very slowly, so that this time it didn't even creak. Down the stairs, stop, listen. The radio was still playing and the kitchen door was shut. Out of the parlour door, round the side of the farmhouse, running, my face on fire. Bobby bounded after me, thinking that I wanted to play, and then the kitchen door opened and there was Janice.

"Just been to the toilet," I muttered, slowing down.

"Oh, Katie," said Janice eagerly, "are you staying to tea? I'm making a raspberry sponge." She was sorry because she'd been so unwelcoming earlier on. Usually Janice and I get on really well, but today I couldn't look at her.

"Umm – Mum wants me – I've got to get back –"

"You and Zillah haven't had an argument, have you? I know what she can be like."

Janice is *so different* from other mothers. She always thinks everything is Zillah's fault.

"No, we're fine, it's just that – I told Mum I'd cook for us, she's painting –"

More lies. Once you start, it's quite hard to stop.

"That's nice. Maggie doesn't know how lucky she is, having you for a daughter."

Why do you say things like that? You even say them in front of Zillah. Do you think it makes me happy? Do you think it makes Zillah happy?

"What are you cooking for tonight?" went on Janice cheerfully. Janice loves talking about food. So do I, usually, so we often have long chats about pasta sauce, or homemade ice cream. Janice says I can make Christmas puddings with her in October. She's got a recipe that's been in her family for more than a hundred years.

October. We won't be here by then. We'll have had to leave the cottage. Janice *knows* I won't be here to make Christmas puddings.

"Um – spag bol – got to go –"

Janice was looking at me worriedly. "Are you sure you're all right, Katie?"

"I'm fine! Everything's great! Bye!" I turned and ran, leaving Janice standing there. If she cared so much about what we were having for our meal, why didn't she care that we wouldn't even have a home to cook it in by October? I ran without stopping, through the yard, down to the gate, down to the lane that led home.

Zillah had known about the plans. She'd known, and she hadn't wanted to tell me. She'd thought she could sort it all out without telling me, but she was wrong.

"Katie!" It was Zillah, running after me. But I didn't slow down. I was in the cross-country team at my London school, and I know how to run.

"Katie!" Her voice was sharp, almost frightened. "Katie! Don't go!"

And I couldn't run away from Zillah. She was my friend. None of this was her fault. I was already slowing down, letting her catch up with me.

"What happened? What did my mum say to you?"

"She didn't say anything. I saw the plans, Zill."

Zillah was silent.

"I saw the Holiday Centre."

"It's not going to happen, Katie!" Zillah burst out. "I'm going to make them stop it."

But I wasn't sure of anything any more.

Chapter Seven

Zillah didn't go back to the farm until eight o'clock. I cooked us spag bol and Zillah made garlic bread. Mum was painting in the studio. I looked in to tell her the spaghetti was ready, but she was sitting in the middle of the floor surrounded by sketches, some of them taped to the floor. She was holding another sketch at arm's length, squinting at it while absentmindedly eating a bar of Milka. Spoiling her appetite with chocolate again.

"Mum!" I shouted quite loudly.

"What?"

"Your meal's on the table."

"Oh, Katie, are you back from school already? What time is it?"

"It's six o'clock and I've made spag bol for all of us. Zillah's here."

"Oh, lovely." Mum smiled a guilty, wheedling smile. "Listen, Katie, would you mind if I ate mine in here, just for once? I'm right in the middle of this – if I stop I'll lose it –"

This was excellent. It meant that Zillah and I could continue our Caravan Park Crisis talks without interruption.

"Oh, all right, Mum. I'll bring your bowl in here. Do you want cheese on it?"

"Thanks, Katie, you're a star."

I hadn't told Mum about the school closing yet. I'd do that later, after Zillah had gone. I brought Mum her spaghetti, garlic bread and a glass of water.

"Mind you eat it straight away, Mum. It'll be horrible cold."

Zillah and I took our food out into the garden. We've got a folding table for the garden now, which Mum bought in a car-boot sale in St Just. We stained the table leaf-green, and I stencilled a border of ivy-leaves around it, and painted them in darker green. We decorated the chairs too. They were broken when we got them, but Mum's fixed some new wooden cross-pieces underneath them so that they don't fold up when you're sitting on them any more.

When we'd finished eating, Zillah got out our crisis planning sheet. First of all we wrote our AIMS AND OBJECTIVES, which is what Mr T tells us to do when we're beginning a school project. "How can you achieve anything if you don't know what you're trying to achieve?" he always says.

Zillah once argued that the man who discovered penicillin didn't know he was looking for it. He just found some mould growing on a piece of bread and thought it might be useful.

"Yes, but the point is that he *thought* about the bread. He didn't just throw it away because it had mould on it," answered Mr T triumphantly.

Imagine Mr T not being head teacher any more. Imagine him not rushing around creating internet links with schools in Yakutsk and Lima. Imagine him not there to tell us that our brains are the best computers of all, and that people would pay a million pounds if our brains were for sale in the shops. Imagine no Assemblies with Mr T telling us funny stories and Mrs Isaacs coughing to remind him that it's time to get on with the next hymn. Imagine someone else living in the Trevelyans' house. No trikes and scooters zooming up and down the hall, no puppy in the doll's pram and no Mrs T hanging up the washing with the baby clinging on to her legs, and waving to me and Zillah over the playground wall. . .

No Mrs T. She wouldn't be here. Mr T would have to get a job somewhere else – maybe right on the other side of Cornwall. Or maybe not even in Cornwall at all.

Don't think about that.

"Zillah, what'll happen to the school buildings?"

Zillah frowned. "I don't know. I suppose they'll be sold."

"Our school's too big for a house."

"Developers buy up big places and turn them into something else."

"You mean a developer like Shift & Partner?"

"Could be." Zillah picked up the last bit of garlic bread and began to nibble it.

"I wonder if it *is* Shift & Partner," I said thoughtfully. "Imagine if they're going to set up holiday centres all round here. They could turn the school into a luxury hotel."

Zillah choked on her garlic bread. "You are joking, Katie?"

"Well, if they did a lot of work they could. There's loads of space – and it's really beautiful round there. People would pay to stay there. They could have a golf driving range on our school field, and a swimming-pool, and a sauna, and maybe even a helicopter pad –"

"We know what our aims and objectives are," said Zillah. "We want to stop the caravan park. That's simple." It sounded simple, the way Zillah said it, but I had a nagging feeling of doubt. "We've got to have an action plan," went on Zillah.

It took ages, and we kept arguing over what to put first, but by the time Mum came stretching and yawning out of the studio, we had our action plan. This is what it looks like.

1) **Photocopy the caravan park plans**. Zillah to take them into school on Wednesday, when G & J go to market. Z to ask Mrs Isaacs if she can do a photocopy, K to ask Mrs Isaacs about her dinner money at the same time so Mrs I doesn't see what Z is copying.

2) Find out as much as we can about **Shift & Partner**. Find out where they are based, and whether they have developed any other caravan parks. Zillah to pretend she is really interested and question G & J. (But will they believe that, after everything Z has already said to them about hating the idea so much?)

3) Find out **how much money J & G are borrowing** to build the caravan park, and when they are going to sign the contracts. "That's really important," said Zillah. "Once they've signed the contracts, then I reckon Shift & Partner can go ahead whatever happens."

4) **Sabotage the plans.**
   "How do we do that?"
   "Blow things up," said Zillah. I stared at her. She was joking, of course. She had to be. "Let down their car tyres, damage their equipment. That sort of thing."
   "But, Zillah, that's against the law."

"Is it? Are you sure?" mocked Zillah.

"Anyway, by then – by the time they start building – it will all be too late. Your parents will have signed the contracts, and Shift & Partner will go ahead whatever happens."

"I know." The fight went out of Zillah, and she looked tired and miserable. "It's like I said before. They've got all the power."

"No..." I said. I was thinking aloud. "Not *all* the power. We've got some too, because we know more about their plans than they think we do. And we can find out even more."

"What about your mum?" asked Zillah.

"What about her?"

"D'you think we should tell her about what they're planning?"

"Zillah! No!"

"She might be able to help."

"No. Janice is her friend. She'd just say, 'Of course, Janice, if you need the cottage, then Katie and I will find somewhere else.' She'd pretend she didn't mind."

Tomorrow I'm going to look for information about Shift & Partner on the internet, and in the phone book and maybe in the St Ives library if Mum'll take me in. I'm also going to phone loads of caravan parks and try to find out about how they were developed, how long it took, how much it cost and so on. Meanwhile Zillah will steal the plans so we can photocopy them, and get as much information as she can out of her mum and dad.

It's going to be a busy day.

Chapter Eight

At nine o'clock we all filed into the Hall for Assembly. Mr T was waiting for us. He was pale and his hair was combed neatly instead of sticking up on end as it usually does. He walked nervously up and down until everyone was settled. Then he smiled his nicest smile.

"I'm glad we're all here," he said. "I've got something sad to tell you, and when you've got sad news you need your friends. All of you are my friends, and you always will be."

And then he told us about the plan to close the school. I hate the word "plan" now. It's turned into something that arrives from outside and doesn't care about what's already there. Mr Trevelyan told us that the Education Department had decided to close our school because they thought that there weren't enough new children coming in every year.

"They say our school will become too small to give you children the kind of education you deserve."

The little Reception children at the front looked up at him. They didn't understand a word, but they like Assembly with Mr Trevelyan. They were waiting for him to make one of his jokes, so that everyone would laugh and they could laugh as well, really loudly, the way little kids do.

Mr Trevelyan talked some more, explaining things to us, and then he said that if we had any questions, he'd try to answer them. Mark put his hand up straight away.

"Where will everyone go, if the school's closed?"

Mark's in Top Group, like us, so he's leaving at the end of this term anyway. But he's got two little cousins in Mrs Isaacs' class. Loads of people in my school are related to one another.

"Each child will be given a place in the primary school closest to his or her home. Apart from those of you who are moving on to secondary school, of course."

"So, we won't all be in the same school any more? All the younger ones, like my cousins – they'll be split up?"

"They'll be going to different schools, yes, depending on where they live."

"Will they keep friends together?"

Mr T cleared his throat. "I'm sorry, Mark. I don't think that will be possible in all cases."

There were lots more questions. *Who will be our teachers? Will you be coming with us, sir? Will Mrs Isaacs be coming?* You could tell that Mr Trevelyan was trying hard not to sound sad, as he explained that he would be looking for another head-teacher's job in another school, and that Mrs Isaacs had decided to take early retirement. And then Zillah put her hand up.

"Mr Trevelyan, what's going to happen to the school buildings?"

Mr Trevelyan looked surprised. All the other questions had been about people.

"Well, Zillah, I'm not entirely sure, but I gather that there's interest in developing the school buildings, along with the schoolhouse."

"What as, sir?"

Mr T looked even more surprised, but he answered Zillah.

"I believe that a holiday and leisure group is interested."

"I *told* you," I whispered, as Zillah put her hand down. "A hotel! I bet you a million pounds it's Shift & Partner!"

After a bit the questions died down. Jenny Pendour started crying noisily, and Mrs Isaacs nodded at Mr T and sat down at the piano. She thumped out a chord and we all began to sing *Colours of Day*, and soon you couldn't hear Jenny at all. Which was a relief, because otherwise everyone might have started to cry.

Nobody talked about anything else. Nobody could *think* about anything else. It was like a storm breaking over our heads. But while the storm raged, Zillah and I carried on with our action plan. We had to. At break-time I told Mrs Isaacs that Mum thought there'd been a mistake about my dinner money because she'd paid for three weeks and I'd been off with a cold one day... Mrs Isaacs sighed and got out the dinner register.

"Can I make some photocopies, Mrs Isaacs? I've got fifty p," said Zillah.

"All right, Zillah... Now, Katie, let's sort this out."

Zillah photocopied furiously while Mrs Isaacs pored over the dinner register.

"I see what it is. You were away on Wednesday, Katie, and that's the day you normally bring packed lunch, so you didn't get a credit for that day."

Zillah was folding the plans, and the photocopies, tucking them away in her backpack.

"Thanks, Mrs Isaacs!"

"That's all right, Zillah. Now, Katie, if you tell your mother that we still owe her one pound fifteen, because of the in-service day the week before last..."

Zillah was waiting for me outside the office.

"OK?"

"Yeah. I'll show you later."

We went out into the playground.

"Katie! Zillah! Come over here!"

Everyone was talking at once.

"They can't do it!"

"We've got to stop them."

"My dad went to this school – and my grandad."

But no one had any real ideas. After a while Zillah and Mark and I wandered over to the playground gate.

"Our parents'll know all about it by now," said Mark. "Mr T said he'd sent letters to them in the post. And my mum –"

But I wasn't listening. A long black car had drawn up on the other side of School Lane. There were two men in it. They didn't get out, they just sat there, staring at the school. Something about them was familiar – I was sure I'd seen them before –

"Zillah! Those two men!"

It *was* them. It was the two men we'd seen measuring in Zillah's fields. They weren't measuring this time, but they weren't just casually looking either. They were *surveying*. They didn't have their instruments this time, but they were giving the school a really professional look-over. A minute later the car's engine started, and they were gone.

"What's the matter?" asked Mark.

Zillah and I looked at each other.

"Katie thinks those men are developers who want to buy our school buildings, once the school's closed down," said Zillah.

I was amazed. Zillah tells me things, but not other people.

"How do you know?" asked Mark.

"We've seen them before."

"Well, they're wasting their time then," said Mark, "because our school's not closing. No one round here's going to let that happen, whatever the Education Department thinks." He sounded so confident. "My dad'll be up here, so will my mum and my uncle and aunt and everyone, and all our village. Same in all the other villages. There'll be hundreds of us, once we get together. No one round here's going to let this school go. We're bound to win."

Suddenly it didn't seem as if the planners had all the power, and we had none. Maybe Mark was right. Maybe everyone had to join together. But Zillah and I were working on our own, trying not to let anyone know what we were doing –

"You wait," said Mark. "We'll have a meeting, a really big meeting. We'll get an action plan. They'll *have* to listen to us."

"Action plan?" asked Zillah.

"Yeah!" Mark was getting really enthusiastic now. "SOS! Save Our School."

But Susie Buryan was listening. "SOS doesn't mean that, Mark," she said bossily. "It means Save Our Souls. We did it at Guides."

"With Susie on our side, we're bound to win," said Zillah.

Chapter Nine

Mum and I have just had hot chocolate with marshmallows. I read the letter Mr T sent to the parents about the school closing, but it didn't say much more than he'd told us.

Mum really surprised me. She wasn't in the studio when I got home, she was at the kitchen table with a stack of paper and envelopes. She had already written to:

1) Our Member of Parliament
2) Our local councillor
3) The Chair of the Education Committee
4) The Minister for Education
5) Mr T (This was a letter of support, Mum said.)

It was strange to see letters addressed to the Houses of Parliament lying on our kitchen table.

"Will they read them, Mum?" I asked.

"Of course they'll read them," said Mum, looking ferocious. "I'm a voter. If enough of us write, they've got to take notice."

I told her about Mark's idea of a big meeting. Mum had a really brilliant idea. "I'll design posters and postcards for the campaign. I know where I can get them printed cheaply. We've got to make a visual impact!"

I'd never known Mum so excited about something that wasn't to do with painting.

"Mum."

"What?"

"Why are you so – I mean, I'm leaving at the end of term anyway – and you don't usually do things at my school..."

Mrs Buryan is always the first to volunteer for a cake stall or to sell raffle tickets, and Mum is always the last.

Mum spun round. "Don't you understand, Katie? That school is the centre of our community. All the farms round here send their children there. If the children get parcelled off to about five different schools, the community won't be the same any more. And besides –"

"What?"

"Well, think how good everyone's been to us, ever since we came. Mrs T coming over with those eggs – that load of wood the Buryans sent – and just think of everything that Janice and Geoff have done. If Janice hadn't offered us the cottage we could never have afforded to live here."

Yes, just think, I thought to myself.

"So if we can do anything to help when there's a crisis like this, we've got to do it."

Mum's face was flushed and determined. As soon as she'd finished her letters, she started sketching out some designs for a poster.

"Don't you want to do that in the studio, Mum?"

"No, these are only roughs. I'm fine in here."

Oh no, you're not, I thought. I'd got loads of phone calls to make, and I definitely couldn't make them with Mum sitting there. I'd found nothing on the internet. Shift & Partner didn't have a website.

"Um – I really want to get on with the cooking, Mum. I need the table."

"Oh dear, Katie, you're doing all the cooking these days. Maybe I should make us some home-made soup, and then I can carry on with this afterwards..."

"No, Mum," I said firmly. I dread Mum's home-made soup. She believes that, if she cooks them long enough, old cabbages, bacon bones, sprouting onions and plenty of cold water will, by a miracle, transform themselves into *delicious, nourishing soup*. "I'll do us scrambled eggs. But I need to clear the kitchen table."

Mum gathered all her stuff together, and disappeared into the studio. I leaped to the phone, with my list of numbers ready.

Conversation 1

Me: Could I speak to the Head of Planning, Mr Carmichael, please?

Receptionist: Have you got an appointment?

Me: No, I only want to speak to him on the phone.

R: I don't think he's in. I don't know where he's gone. What's it about?

Me: I want to ask him about planning permission for caravan parks.

R: You got a caravan park?

Me: No. I just want to find out about them.

R: (with suspicion) Is it for one of those school projects?

Me: No! It's not a project! It's real life.

R: 'Cos we get pestered to death with those school projects. Anyway, he's not here.

Me: Is there anyone else I could ask?

R: Could try Mrs Bucket, I suppose. (*I think that's what she said – but the name can't really have been Bucket, can it?*)

RING RING RING RING RING. NO ANSWER.

R: Looks like she's gone as well. It's quite late, you know.

Me: It's only quarter to five.

R: Well, they have long journeys, you know. And Mrs Bucket comes in on her bike.

Me: I DON'T CARE IF SHE COMES ON HER

BROOMSTICK. (*No, I didn't say it aloud.*) What's the best time to call tomorrow?

R: Ooh, I couldn't really say. They're busy people, you know. Are you *sure* it's not for one of those school projects?

Me: !!!!!!!! ****** !!!!!!!!

Conversation 2 (With radio playing loudly and little kids screaming in the background.)

Caravan Park Owner: Ullo! Ullo! I can't hear you!

Me: I'm calling to ask about how you started to develop your caravan park.

CPO: (bellowing) This is Golden Cove Caravan Park! Can you hear me?

Me: Yes, I can hear you. Can you hear me? I WANT TO ASK YOU ABOUT SETTING UP A CARAVAN PARK.

CPO: You want to rent a caravan site? Sorry, my lover, we're full up.

Me: NO, I DON'T WANT TO RENT A CARAVAN SITE.

CPO: Then what you calling me for? Do your mum and dad know you're making this phone call? You're wasting my time, you are.

Me: No, I'm not wasting your time, I really want to know. I've got some friends who want to set up a caravan park—

CPO: Yeah, at the bottom of their garden along with

the fairies, I daresay. You clear off and don't bother me no more, or I'll do 1471 and tell your mum and dad.

SLAM from CPO's phone. SLAM from our phone. Even though there's no one else in the kitchen, my face is bright red.

Conversation 3
Tourist Development Officer: What exactly do you mean when you say "caravan park"? Do you mean a mobile home site, or a holiday caravan site, a site with full facilities or a field with a Portaloo? I can't help you unless you can be more specific. Do you require this information for a school pro—
Me: No! No! It's not a school project. I just want to know. What about if it was a caravan park which took up about six fields, and a cottage as a Holiday Centre, and a café and a toilet-block and a shower-block and—
TDO: How big are the fields?
Me: Quite small – well, medium-sized, really.
TDO: And what is the location? That will affect the value of the land.
Me: It's a farm by the sea.
TDO: Just a moment. A farm by the sea, you say. Are you quite sure it's not in an Area of Outstanding Natural Beauty? Or an Area of Special Scientific Interest?

Me: ????

TPO: (very severely) You can't just go putting caravan sites wherever you like, you know. These things have to be properly approved. There are a huge number of factors to be taken into account.

Me: So you might not be allowed to do it?

TPO: I'm not saying that.

Me: !!!!!!!! ****** !!!!!!!! ******

The trouble is that people in offices won't take you seriously if you sound young. And it's not until I was halfway through talking to them that I realized I wasn't asking the right questions. But then I realized something else. Janice and Geoff must have had to find out all these things too. And the officers would have talked to them. I grabbed the phone and called Zillah.

Conversation 4

Me: Zill? I've just thought. Your parents must have talked to the planning people, and the tourism people, and other caravan park owners. You could ask what they said.

Z: They won't tell me anything. They stop talking every time I come into the kitchen. And I'm not talking to them, anyway.

Me: Zillah, you've *got to try*. Pretend you've changed. You're really interested and excited about the caravan park now. Tell them you only didn't like it at first because you were worried about me, but now you know we can easily find another cottage, so you don't mind. Say you want to work in the caravan-park café!

Z: They'll never believe it. . .

Me: They will. They will, because they'll *want* to believe it. You know how your mum hates it when you won't talk to her.

Z: OK then. I'll try. But listen, Katie –

Me: What?

Z: *You* want to work in the caravan park too. Maybe a cleaning job in the toilet-block?

Me: !!!!!!!! ****** !!!!!!!!

Chapter Ten

So much is happening. The phone rings all the time. Mum's finished her poster design and she's going down to St Ives tomorrow to get the posters printed as a rush job. The printer's not even charging her anything, because he used to go to our school when he was young. He says he wants to support SOS. That's what we're called now: the Save Our School Action Group, SOS for short. You can see why we didn't want to call it SOSAG for short – think of the endless sausage jokes.

School was buzzing with plans all yesterday and all today. I wanted to ask Mrs T about her interview with the Chair of the Education Committee, but she wasn't in her garden and the house looked empty and quiet. Loads of parents have signed up for SOS, and all the children are junior members. Everyone's writing down what they can do for the campaign on a huge sheet of paper that's on the table outside Mr T's office. We're collecting signatures for a petition from all the old pupils too. A writer who rents a cottage from Mark's dad is writing an article about SOS for the *St Ives Times & Echo*, and maybe for *The Cornishman* as well. He's interviewing everyone tomorrow.

Zillah's found out loads of stuff from her parents about the caravan park. They believed her straight away when she said she'd changed her mind. I knew they would. They were *so grateful* to Zillah for not hating them any more. I managed to talk to Mrs Bucket on the phone at last (yes, she does exist, and that *is* her name), but she wasn't very helpful. And I saw Granny Carne again.

Meeting Granny Carne was the most important thing. I put it last because I'm still thinking about it.

I met Granny Carne in our lane, as I was going home from the school bus stop. I'd said goodbye to Zillah, and I was walking slowly, looking over the gates at the fields and trying to imagine how they'd look when they were full of caravans. And our cottage was going to be the holiday centre, so hundreds of people would be going up and down this lane, getting the keys to their caravans, asking questions, buying maps and canisters of camping gas. But it was hard to believe that it could happen, when everything was warm and summery and still.

A cow lowed at me as I looked over the gate, and a wren fluttered into the hedge. I stood still and listened. I could hear cows munching grass, a dog barking – probably Bobby barking with excitement because Zillah was home – the soft sound of the wind and the far-off shushing of the sea. And the noise of a tractor. Lots of quiet sounds that belonged here. Janice and Geoff were planning to make a car park. They'd have to tarmac over one of the fields. There'd be the growl of car engines, and the smell of petrol fumes. I shut my eyes to imagine it better. I could almost see the glitter and flash of the sun on car windscreens and caravans. I could almost hear the excited screaming of children, smell the burgers from Janice and Geoff's café, and watch visitors pouring into the holiday centre. They would never know that the room where they were queuing for their keys used to be Mum's studio.

I opened my eyes, and there were the quiet fields running down to the cliff. Was it really going to happen? I wished I could look into the future, just for a second –

And suddenly she was there, as I came round the bend in the lane. Granny Carne. She didn't look at all surprised to see me. In fact, she looked as if she'd been waiting for me. There's nothing mysterious about that, I told myself. The school bus drops me off at the lane-end at about the same time every afternoon. You don't have to be able to foretell the future to know that.

"Hello, Katie."

"Hello."

She had her hands thrust deep into her pockets. The sun was hot, but she was wearing a long skirt, boots and jacket, with a bright red scarf tied over her hair. Her clothes were old and faded, the colours of lichen and moss. Only her scarf leaped with colour. Suddenly I remembered the sweet taste of the water from her spring, and I swallowed. My mouth was dry.

"You thirsty, Katie? It's a hot day, sure enough. You'll have to come and drink some of my water again. But you're busy. I can tell from the look of you. Lots of things crowding around in your mind, aren't there?"

"Yes."

"You're busy worrying about all of them. What are Zillah's mum and dad going to do? What's Zillah going to do? What's your mum going to do? What's happening with the school? All that's going around in your mind. Let them sort themselves out, girl. Question is, what are *you* going to do?"

It sounded like an accusation.

"I *am* trying," I said. "But people don't listen to you, if you're young."

"Maybe they don't. But you can listen to yourself. Listen to what you really want. Why don't you try that first?"

I didn't know what she meant. How can you listen to yourself?

"You listen to yourself, and then other people'll listen to you," said Granny Carne. Now that I was standing right next to her, I realized how tall she was. As tall as my dad was, nearly. And straight up, like a tree. Not like an old woman at all. A grey and green and brown tree with a bright crown of colour.

"I'll be off home," she said. "You know what they used to call us, Katie, years ago, 'cos we lived up on the Downs? They used to call us mountainy people. That's 'cos they never saw any real mountains."

"I've seen mountains. Me and my dad climbed to the top of Ben Nevis when we went to Scotland, not last summer but the summer before."

"There you are then. You've got something to make a comparison. Most of the time people see their own little hills and they call them mountains. They can't see over them and they can't see around them." And she was away, striding up the lane.

Question is, what are you going to do? I leaned on the gate and thought about it. The sounds slowly filled my ears. A dog barking – not Bobby this time. A pair of gulls wheeling and calling in the summer sky. The chunter of a tractor setting off along the road. I listened. What did I want?

I wanted to stay here.

Yes, I wanted to stay in our cottage if we could, but even if Janice and Geoff told us to leave, I wanted to stay around here. We could get another cottage.

But that meant I couldn't hide things from Mum any more. She'd got to know, because October was less than four months away. If we were going to find somewhere else to live, we'd have to start looking soon.

I stood there, thinking and listening. That was when a voice floated out of the past to me. It was Zillah's voice, from back when we first met, last year: "*She put it in her will. It's there in black and white, whatever Dad says. She left me the cottage as well. The cottage where you're living. 'To my great-niece and namesake, Zillah, in loving remembrance.'*"

The cottage was Zillah's. Her great-aunt had left it to her. So surely Geoff and Janice couldn't turn it into a holiday centre, after all? Why hadn't Zillah thought of that? Maybe Zillah and I were seeing mountains where there was only a little hill. Granny Carne was right. I should have listened more.

Conversation 5

Me: (panting with excitement at my discovery) Zillah? Listen, your mum and dad can't turn the cottage into a holiday centre. Your Great-aunt Zillah left it to you.

Z: (not excited at all) I know.

Me: Did you forget?

Z: No.

Me: ???

Z: (long silence, then a flat, quiet voice) Thing is, Katie, though she did leave it to me, it's in trust till I'm twenty-one. That means Mum and Dad look after it for me. Mum says the law says they've got to "administer it in the way that is of most benefit to me". She reckons that getting money from the holiday centre is of most benefit to me. The caravan park is going to pay me a proper rent for the cottage. Mum says it's all legal.

Me: Oh.

Z: I know. I thought I could stop them using it, but I can't. Katie –

Me: What?

Z: My mum cried when I told her I'd changed my mind about the caravan park. She was that pleased.

Me: Oh.

Z: I felt awful. (Another long silence.) 'Cos now I know they're in big trouble.

Me: What sort of trouble?

Z: Shift & Partner have lied to my mum and dad. They've told them they don't need to bother about the planning office or the tourism office or anything. All they have to do is sign the loan contracts and Shift & Partner will sort everything out. So my mum and dad don't really know anything. They don't know much more than we do. Katie, *how can they be so stupid?*

Zillah's voice was full of pain. I couldn't think what to say. Zillah didn't get on too well with her parents, but she was proud of them in her way.

"You know what you said before," I started cautiously. "Your mum and dad are farmers, not business people. It's not their fault."

"Shift & Partner are crooks!" said Zillah fiercely. "They're after my mum and dad's land, that's what it is. What if we can't pay back the loans? We'll lose the farm. My mum told me the farm was their security for the loans. That farm's all my mum and dad ever wanted. It's their life. That's why they went for this stupid caravan park business, because they think it'll help them to keep the farm going."

"Zillah, how much are the loans? Do you know?"

"I'm not sure. But I asked Mum how much it takes to set up the caravan park. She said it's a lot of money at first – it's called *capital outlay*. But once the caravan park gets going it will make loads of money, and they'll be able to pay the loans back and make a profit as well. That's what Shift & Partner have told them."

"How much do you think they'll need to borrow, then?"

"I think it's about a hundred thousand pounds," said Zillah.

"A hundred thousand pounds!"

"I know. And then they have to pay fifteen per cent interest a year on top of it, so that's fifteen thousand pounds. And it's all secured against the farm, so if Mum and Dad can't pay, Shift & Partner can take possession of our farm. I just can't believe that Mum and Dad don't see that they're crooks."

I remembered the long black car sliding to a stop outside our school. I remembered the two men looking. Surveying. Wanting. They wanted property. They wanted our school, and they wanted Zillah's parents' land. The caravan park was part of it, but it was only a small part. It was their way of getting to what they wanted.

"Maybe – maybe Shift & Partner don't really mind if your parents can't pay back the loans," I said.

"What do you mean?"

"The caravan park could just be a way of getting your mum and dad to borrow money from Shift & Partner. Maybe they know those loans can't ever be paid. And then they'll get the farm."

"But what would they want our farm for? Farms don't make money, not round here."

"No, I know. But they could turn it into something else. They'd have all the land. Another big hotel, or a leisure centre. Something that would really make money."

"My mum and dad would never believe it. They don't think like that."

"Then we've got to make them. Listen Zillah, I'm going to tell my mum."

"You can't!"

"I've got to. We could be homeless, Zillah. And maybe my mum can make your parents understand about Shift & Partner."

"Nobody can," said Zillah gloomily.

"They haven't signed yet, have they? The loan contracts, I mean."

"No. Not yet."

Chapter Eleven

But a lot of things happened before I was able to talk to Mum. After I'd finished my phone call to Zillah, the cottage was still and quiet. I'd left the front door wide open, because it gets too warm in the kitchen otherwise, with the stove lit. (We have to keep the stove going, even in summer, because we cook on it.)

A lot had happened, but my mind wasn't rushing and racing any more. I was thinking step by step. Tell Mum. Talk to Mrs T. Find out more about Shift & Partner. It was all becoming clearer.

And then I heard a sound. Car tyres, crunching and crackling on the rough stones of the lane. Mum nearly always leaves our van up at the top of the lane, because when it rains our tyres get stuck in the mud. But it didn't sound like the van. The engine noise was richer, almost like a purr.

I heard the brakes, then the engine was switched off. One door slammed, then another. Mum's voice came into my head.

"Put the bolt across the door, Katie, when I'm out. Just in case."

The door was wide-open. A moment later a shadow filled the doorway. A dark shape, blocking out the sunlight, with another shape following behind it.

"Anyone home?" He was pushing through the doorway as if our cottage belonged to him. I stood up.

"It's the kid, Jason," he said, as if he knew who I was. "You all on your own, are you?"

I took a deep breath, walked to the doorway, and stood there blocking it. "No, my mum's upstairs, having a rest. She's got a headache. Did you want something?"

"Did I want something? Well, there's a question." His mouth opened and I saw his teeth. I think it was meant to be a smile. Jason turned aside and began to whistle. "We're just taking a little look around," said the man in the doorway. "That all right with you?" He said it mockingly, the way some people talk to children as if nothing they do or say can really matter.

I didn't answer. I could tell they were going to do what they wanted, anyway.

"Maybe we can have a chat with your mum later. When she wakes up from her little rest."

"What did you want to look at?"

"Oh, this and that. Here and there. The general

picture, that's what we want. If that's all right with you. And your mum."

Jason stopped whistling. "Let's get on with it, Ludo."

Ludo! You might as well call someone Snakes & Ladders, I thought.

Ludo stared at me hard. "Find my name amusing, do you?"

"No—"

"It's short for Ludovic. Vic for Victory. It's a very nice name. Isn't it a very nice name?"

"Oh, leave it out, Ludo," said Jason.

They both stepped back out into the sunshine. Behind them, the windscreen of their low, long black car winked and glittered in the light. Ludo shaded his eyes and looked out and away, at the fields which ran down to the sea, and the cliffs, and the wrinkled line of coast with the dark-blue sea beyond.

"People'd pay a million pounds for a view like this," he observed.

"Lovely," said Jason.

"Soon be lots of happy caravanners enjoying it, eh, Jason?" And he winked. He thought I hadn't noticed.

At that moment I knew for sure that Zillah was right. Shift & Partner didn't want a caravan park, any more than we did. They had no interest in it at all. "Happy caravanners" was just a joke. They had other plans. Maybe a big hotel, maybe luxury summer homes. Something *they* knew about, but Janice and Geoff didn't. The Treliskes wouldn't know their real plans until Shift & Partner had got hold of the farm. Shift & Partner thought we were all stupid enough to believe anything, and so far they'd been right. They thought I was so stupid they could wink in front of me and I wouldn't notice. And that was when I got angry, and said the stupidest thing I've ever said to anyone.

"You want to buy our school as well, don't you?"

Ludo whipped round to face me. "What do you mean?"

"I saw you looking at it. We all did. Do you want to build a caravan park up there as well?"

"Why, you little—"

"Take it easy, Ludo," said Jason again, more urgently this time. Ludo bent forward, leaning over me.

"You want to watch what you're saying," he said quietly.

"Yeah, that's libel, that is," added Jason, but I wasn't afraid of him. It was Ludo's quiet voice that slid into me like ice. I moved backwards, just a little, but he moved with me.

"About time you woke your mum up from her little sleep," he said. "I want a word with her. I've got a good removal firm I can recommend."

"But we're not moving house," I said. I was beginning to feel afraid.

"Oh, I think you are. Your mum's friendly with the people up at the farm, isn't she? I've heard all about it. I know who *you* are. Letting you stay here for free, aren't they? Very nice. But they can't be giving you their charity any more. It's not convenient. Mr and Mrs Treliske are too nice to come down themselves and tell you to move on. So we've come instead. Go and wake your mum up."

The sun shone brightly. It was a perfect afternoon in summer. In a minute everything would go back to normal and I'd be able to talk and move again instead of standing frozen, staring at the white teeth that showed through Ludo's parted lips. Jason coughed, and turned aside.

"Go on," said Ludo, more quietly than ever.

And suddenly she was there. She hadn't gone back up the hill that wasn't really a mountain. She was standing right beside the low, long black car, watching us.

"Granny Carne!"

Jason and Ludo turned. Granny Carne looked taller than ever, like a tree I could shelter under. "You all right there, Katie?" she asked.

"My mum –" I said, in a squeaky voice that was strange to me. "These men –"

"Don't be frightened, Katie. Your mum's on her way. Time I was at the top of the lane, I saw this car turn down here. Your mum doesn't have visitors with cars like this 'un. So I thought I'd take a little dander down and see what was doing."

"Well, you can dander up again. Keep out of it. This is none of your business," said Ludo angrily. "And you're on private land."

"This lane's a right of way," said Granny Carne firmly. "Has been for hundreds of years. You won't stop that. People've got the right to walk free."

"We'll soon see about that."

"Yes, we'll see," said Granny Carne. She looked as if she could see a long way, right past Jason and Ludo. Without realizing it, I'd drawn close to her so I was standing right beside her. I felt safer, but still a bit afraid.

"I wish your mother could see you now," Granny Carne said to Ludo. She didn't say it angrily, but as if she pitied him. "Wanted you to be a lawyer, didn't she? That's why she gave you that name. Ludovic. Thought it'd look good on top of some posh letter-paper."

"How do you –" he hissed, through shut teeth.

"That's right, your mother paid a lot to put you through that college, didn't she?" went on Granny Carne. "Lucky she never knew where that money really went. She was so proud of you. She died proud of you, that's something. She never knew you like you are now."

Ludo was white. I thought for a second that he'd go for her, maybe hit her or something to stop the words coming out of her mouth. But her face stopped him. Maybe it was the sadness in it.

"You get along home," she said. "And take him along with you." She nodded at Jason. "You don't belong here, either of you."

I stayed close to Granny Carne as Ludo and Jason got into their car and slammed the doors shut. The engine growled and the tyres spat out stones as their car surged up the lane. They were gone.

"Did you know them?" I asked.

"In a manner of speaking," said Granny Carne. "I'll be getting back now. You'll be all right, Katie. Your mother's on her way home."

Chapter Twelve

The Council of War

Mum was on her way home all right. I soon heard the van rattling and banging its way down the lane. Why was she bringing it all the way down here, when she's always saying the engine will fall to pieces if it gets shaken about much more? The din rose to a crescendo as Mum parked the van in front of the cottage.

"Silencer's gone!" she yelled through the window.

"Hi Mum! Hi Mrs T!"

It was wonderful to see them. The baby who isn't really a baby any more was bellowing in his car seat. And there, crouched in the back of the van, was Zillah. They must have stopped at the farm to bring her down.

"We're here for a council of war, Katie," said Mrs T. "SOS is holding a big public meeting on Friday night. Maggie and I are going to deliver leaflets about it to every house and farm in the area. We've got to get hundreds of people at that meeting!"

Mum and Mrs T looked at each other, their eyes sparkling.

"We're going to win this one!" said Mrs T. Then she twisted round to try and unhitch the baby from his straps. He grabbed her hair and pulled a lump of it hard.

"Ow! Blast! *Calm down, I'm trying to get you out!* Oh, thank you, Katie. Hold him tight or he'll kick you. I think car seats were invented as instruments of torture for mothers –"

The baby stopped yelling as soon as Mrs T passed him out of the van to me. He beamed angelically, reached up and patted my hair as gently as a kitten.

"You ungrateful little monster," said Mrs T. "I think I'll leave you here with Katie, and go off round the world."

I laughed, but Mum was out of the car too, and looking at me hard.

"Are you all right, Katie? You look awful. Has something happened?"

"No, I'm all right, it was just –"

But I couldn't say it. Suddenly, now Ludo and Jason had gone, I was afraid I was going to cry. Ludo's cold, quiet voice clung to me, and echoed in my head. *They can't be giving you their charity any more.* Was he right? Was it charity? And what if Granny Carne hadn't come –?

"There *is* something wrong!" Mum insisted.

"Let's go inside," said Mrs T.

And that's how our council of war began, with Mum and Mrs T on one side of the kitchen table, and Zillah and me on the other. Mum put a clothes horse round the stove so the baby couldn't get near it, and found a roll of wallpaper and some wax crayons for him.

We told them everything. Well, perhaps not quite everything. I certainly wasn't going to tell Mum what Ludo had said about the Treliskes giving us charity, so I didn't tell her that Shift & Partner had come to our cottage. I didn't really want to talk about it anyway, because it would make all the things they'd said more real. And how could I explain properly about Granny Carne? I'd tell Zillah everything later.

Zillah took the plans she'd copied out of her backpack, and we spread them out on the table to look at them. Mum traced the little boxes with her finger, and measured out the distances. She understood the plans straight away. She stared in silence for a long time at the little box marked *Holiday Centre*. At last she said, very quietly, as if she was thinking aloud.

"You can't blame Janice and Geoff. They've had such a hard time. Up at five every morning for years, working all the hours God sends, and still struggling."

I think she'd forgotten that Zillah was there. Zillah's eyes were dark with thought, but she didn't look angry. She was listening intently.

"No," said Mrs T briskly, "you can't blame them, but you can't let them go ahead. Zillah and Katie are right. This whole thing stinks. Those Shift & Partner characters aren't in this to help Zillah's parents. They sound a pretty sinister pair to me. Hang on, let me try and work out these figures. Zillah, can you give them to me again?"

We got pens and paper and my calculator, and started trying to work out what income the caravan park might bring in, and whether it would cover the cost of the loans. Suddenly Mrs T dropped her pen and jumped up.

"What a fool I am. I never thought of Clare Sale. Could I use your phone, Maggie? I'm going to ring one of our parents. You know Robbie Sale, Zillah? His family have got a caravan park."

On the phone, Mrs T's voice sounded clearer and posher than ever. "Is that Clare? Hello, it's Annie Trevelyan, from the school. No, nothing's wrong at all, the meeting's going ahead. I'm just ringing to pick your brains. I've got a friend who's thinking of setting up a caravan park, but she's not sure about whether it'll work. It would be wonderful to have your advice." She went on talking for ages, asking loads of questions and jotting things down on her piece of paper. It all looked amazingly professional, except that the baby kept trying to climb up her legs, until Zillah and I got down on the floor with him and drew a train-track and a train. After that he was perfectly happy, going round in circles making choo-choo noises.

At last, Mrs T finished her call and sat down again, frowning over her piece of paper.

"It's even worse than I thought," she said. "Shift & Partner have misled your parents quite seriously, Zillah. I can't believe it wasn't deliberate. The caravan park will never be able to pay off such a huge loan. Clare Sale says their caravan park costs a fortune to run. They have health-and-safety inspectors coming round all the time and telling them they've got to improve the showers or put in safety rails or fence off the car park. And the last two summers have been appalling for visitors, with all the rain we've had. People have been going abroad for their holidays. Here are the figures Clare's given me."

We all looked at them. I didn't take in all the detail, but it was easy to see that the income figure wasn't much bigger than the expenses figure.

"Clare says she wishes now that they'd just stuck to a few caravans and tents in a field," said Mrs T. "What a nightmare. We've *got* to tell your parents, Zillah, before they sign anything."

Before they sign anything...

Janice and Geoff thought Shift & Partner had arranged everything for them. They thought Shift & Partner had checked the caravan park with the tourist board and the planning people, and probably the health-and-safety people and everyone else. They thought Shift & Partner were genuine. And now they believed that Zillah wanted a caravan park too, because I'd told Zillah to pretend that she'd changed her mind. There was nothing to stop them from signing those loan agreements as soon as Shift & Partner came again.

As soon as Shift & Partner came again.

But they were here. Their long black car was in the neighbourhood. They'd driven back up the lane, but how far had they gone? They'd be in a hurry now. They'd want to get everything fixed up before any more people got suspicious about them.

"Zillah! Quick! We've got to get to your house *now*, before Shift & Partner do. Before your mum and dad sign!"

The baby began to roar.

Chapter Thirteen

We pounded up the lane. Zillah hadn't hesitated for a second. She didn't ask why I thought Shift & Partner might be at the farm. We were out of the door and running, side by side.

The farmyard gate was open, and a long, low black car was drawn up by the parlour door.

"They're here already!"

"They'll be in the kitchen."

Bobby leaped and barked as Zillah pushed open the kitchen door. It was dark inside, after the brightness of the summer day. We blinked, and there they were. Jason, Ludo, Geoff and Janice, two on one side of the kitchen table, two on the other. They were having their own council of war.

There were papers spread on the table in front of them, but they weren't plans this time. They were thick, legal-looking papers, like the will Mum made last year.

"Mum! Dad! Don't!" panted Zillah. But Ludo was staring at me.

"Come to make sure you keep your cottage?" he asked, as if I was a beggar and he already owned the farm.

"It's not that!" I started angrily, but Zillah interrupted. She'd seen what I hadn't seen. She'd seen that her father had a pen in his hand.

"Don't sign, Dad! Wait! They're lying to you!"

"That's libel, that is," said Jason automatically.

"Shut it, Jason," said Ludo. He went on quietly and silkily, talking to Zillah's parents now, and not to us. "This your little girl, is it? I'm afraid she's got into bad company with the other one. Very nasty things young Katie's been saying about you. *They wouldn't dare turn us out of this cottage. My mum says we'll squat if they try. We'll get the law on them.*"

Janice stared at me. "Squat? Get the law on us?"

"Oh, yes, you've got some nice friends down there. *They* don't care about you and your husband, it's a free cottage they're after. So her mum's put her up to spoiling your new business before it's even got started."

"*Don't sign, Dad!*" said Zillah again. Her hand hovered by his. I could tell that she was struggling not to grab the pen. "It's not true about Katie. Katie and her mum would never do a thing like that to us. Shift & Partner are trying to get your land. They know you won't be able to pay off the loans."

Geoff looked from me to Ludo, and back again, and then at Zillah. The pen was still in his hand. "Is this the truth what you're telling me, girl? Katie's not told you what to say?"

"Of course she hasn't!" flashed Zillah. "I've got a mind of my own, haven't I?"

But it was the wrong thing to say.

"Oh yes, my girl, you most certainly have," said Janice. Ludo gave an understanding chuckle. "Now listen here, Zill," Janice went on, "this is grown-up business, important business. It's not for you to tell your dad what he should do, nor me neither."

"That's the way," said Ludo, but now *he'd* said the wrong thing as well. Janice shot him a look, pure and deadly: "*I'll manage my own daughter in my own fashion, thank you.*"

Ludo looked at his watch. "Time's getting on," he said. "If we're going to get these documents lodged with the lawyers tonight, and get the money released to you –"

Geoff pulled the papers towards him. He read over a paragraph, frowning. I knew he wasn't sure. He didn't look happy. He looked at Janice, then at Zillah. He cleared his throat, and read over the passage again. I knew he was trying to gain time. Maybe Geoff wasn't really sure about the papers they were asking him to sign. Maybe he'd never been sure. He wanted a way out of all the hard times he and Janice had had on the farm, and he'd thought for a while that the way out was written on Shift & Partner's papers. Suddenly, without meaning to, I felt sorry for Geoff.

And then I heard the sound I'd been listening for. The racket of an exhaust which had lost its silencer, coming up the lane.

"What in the world is that?" asked Janice.

The noise stopped. Two doors slammed. Footsteps ran towards the door, and the bellowing of an angry baby grew louder and louder.

"It's them!" I whispered to Zillah, and then there was a loud knocking on the door.

"Oh dear, more visitors," said Janice helplessly.

"Sign," said Ludo, leaning forward over the table. "Sign there."

Geoff looked up from the papers. He stared straight at Ludo with the long, scanning look he gives to a cow that kicks out at milking. Then he scanned Zillah, just the same. Then me.

"Open that door, Janice," he said. Then he turned back to Ludo. "I don't reckon we need to rush this. That money'll still be there in the bank tomorrow, and the day after."

"Sign," repeated Ludo, as if he hadn't heard. His lips were slightly parted, and his teeth showed.

"I don't believe I will, just now," said Geoff, and put down his pen and pushed the papers aside. He got up slowly and deliberately from the table, just as Janice let Mum and Mrs T into the kitchen.

"The van wouldn't start," panted Mum.

"Are we in time?" asked Mrs T urgently.

The baby stopped screaming, and looked round at Geoff and Janice, Ludo and Jason, and Zillah and me.

"Yes," said Geoff, "I reckon you're in time. But it's the girls we've got to thank, isn't it, Mr Shift?"

Chapter Fourteen

It's the girls we've got to thank.

Maybe. But not much thanking went on after Shift & Partner had vanished in a splatter of farm-dust and a disappointed growl of exhaust. No one said anything for a while. Janice sagged in her chair, staring at Geoff as if she couldn't believe what had happened. Then her face crumpled.

"What're we going to do now," she said. "We're back where we were, and with everyone knowing our private business on top of it." I felt myself go red. Janice didn't want me there, knowing all about the papers and what she and Geoff had been planning. And Mum knew, and Mrs T as well –

Janice's voice sounded stretched to breaking-point. "What're we going to do," she repeated, but it wasn't a question. Janice didn't believe that anyone in the room would have an answer. She got up clumsily, as if she couldn't see properly, and pushed her way out of the kitchen. We heard her feet clattering on the stairs.

"She's upset," said Geoff. "It's been a shock to her. Been a shock to me too, I don't mind saying it. We thought all our troubles were over. I'll be going to Penzance first thing in the morning to find a lawyer to look at these papers. Should have done that in the first place. But they said they'd carried out all the checks for us."

"I'm sorry, Dad," said Zillah. I knew she didn't mean she was sorry for what we'd done. She didn't wish we'd let Shift & Partner cheat her parents. But she was sorry, all the same, and so was I, because of us knowing their private business, and Janice running out of the room to cry, and Geoff sitting so heavily at the kitchen table, staring ahead at more years of getting up at five in the morning and never being able to pay off the farm's debts.

"Thing is, I wanted to trust them," Geoff went on. "We wanted it all to happen so bad, we didn't ask questions."

"Shall I make us all a cup of tea?" said Mum. "I know where everything is. I'll take one up to Janice in a minute."

"You do that," said Geoff. "She'll need her friends round her at a time like this." The way he smiled at Mum, I knew he hadn't believed it about Mum trying to keep hold of a free cottage.

"I've been saving up the rent," Mum went on as she made the tea. "Even though Janice wouldn't take it, I've put it aside every week. It's all in the post office, waiting. And this time there's to be no argument about it. I'm renting the cottage for a proper rent, and that's that."

"There'll be no argument from me," said Geoff. "You're a good neighbour, Maggie."

"Right, then," said Mum. "I'll take this tea up to Janice."

Mrs T handed round the mugs, while I held the baby. His eyelids were drooping. Suddenly, he gave a huge yawn, and fell asleep. I cuddled him close. He was warm and soft, and a bit damp ... more than a bit damp ... oh no, his nappy was leaking –

Mrs T passed me a plastic carrier-bag.

"Stick this under him," she said. "I simply can't change him now, poor darling, he'll go ballistic. Imagine being a baby, Katie. Or better still, don't. It's lucky that people forget about being babies once they grow up, isn't it?"

I slid the carrier-bag underneath the baby.

"Time for another council of war," said Mrs T. "Mr Treliske, I've got a friend who runs a caravan park—"

"Don't ever let me hear those words again," said Geoff, in a voice of doom.

"And now she wishes she'd never got into it," went on Mrs T, as if she hadn't heard him. "She has more rules and regulations to cope with than paying visitors."

"Go on," said Geoff sarcastically, "give us the rest of the good news."

Mrs T grinned at him. "You don't think there is any, do you? BUT – she said that before they expanded, when she kept things simple, she did quite well. She used to have about a dozen caravans in a field, along with some tents, and she did cream teas. It was quite profitable, apparently."

"We could help with the teas!" I said. I could just see it: a room full of people eating cream teas, smiling and leaving tips for Zillah and me in a saucer. They would love Janice's delicious home-made scones and cakes: she wouldn't have to send them all to the WI sales any more. And the parlour would make a brilliant tea-room – Janice and Geoff never used the parlour anyway – maybe I could even persuade them to get rid of the sulky red cabbage-rose wallpaper and paint the walls white to give an impression of space –

"I can just see our Zillah handing round the tea-cups," said Geoff. "Eh, Zill?"

Zillah scowled. "I'd drop the trays," she said.

I had to admit that was likely. Zillah would be thinking about the book she was reading ... or about tide-tables ... anything but the tray in her hands...

"Zillah could do the bills, and take bookings," said Mrs T firmly. "Her maths is excellent."

"Better than mine, I daresay," said Geoff, sounding sunk in gloom again.

"Of course I didn't mean that," said Mrs T briskly. "They're a very plausible pair, Shift & Partner. No wonder you and Janice got drawn in. I bet they've deceived people up and down the country."

Plausible. I would look it up on Mum's computer thesaurus later on. I was pretty sure that Zillah's dad didn't know what it meant either, but he began to look more cheerful.

"My grandad kept a few caravans in High Field, back before the war," he said thoughtfully. "He did all right with them, as far as I remember. Mind you, my granny used to do breakfasts, as well as high teas. And they used to have artists staying in rooms in the house. Some years the family used to be camping out in the garden to make room for the visitors. But it got them through. No reason it shouldn't get us through... Well, what do you say, girl?"

Zillah flushed. Her father was asking her opinion. He really wanted to know what she thought.

"I reckon we *could* do it, all of us together," said Zillah slowly. "I'll do the bookings, like Mrs T said."

"I'll go on up and tell your mum," said Geoff, standing up in his lumpy, porridge-coloured, Janice-darned socks. (Geoff always takes off his boots outside the kitchen door, and walks around in his socks indoors.)

As soon as he'd gone out of the door, Mrs T sighed deeply, leaned back in her chair, and shut her eyes. Zillah and I looked at each other.

"Are you all right, Mrs T?"

She nodded, without speaking. I had a horrible feeling that if she did speak, she might cry, like Janice. Suddenly I realized that I'd never even asked her how her meeting with the Chair of the Education Committee had gone. There had been too many things in my head. But if the school was closed, Mr T would lose his job, and all the Trevelyans would lose their home.

The plastic bag crackled as the baby began to wake up. But for once, miraculously, he didn't start to cry. He'd have to be changed soon, but I didn't want to disturb Mrs T.

Mrs T opened her eyes. She didn't look if she was going to cry now. Perhaps I'd been mistaken.

"Mrs T, what happened about the Education Committee person you were going to meet?"

"He wasn't there. The secretary said that he'd been called away to an urgent meeting."

"Oh. So you didn't see anyone?"

"No."

I thought of the smart, slightly-too-large suit, and Mrs T's mother taking the little ones to St Ives for the day. Anyone who knows the three little Ts would call that an act of heroism, even if she *is* their grandma. What a waste. By mistake, I said it aloud.

"No, it most certainly was *not*," said Mrs T. "It was just what I needed. You can't blame the secretary, poor thing, she was crimson. Not a good liar at all. It made me *absolutely determined* that they're not going to get away with it. They are going to *have to listen to us.* They can't hide behind secretaries and receptionists all the time. We've all heard quite enough blather about 'economic viability', and 'overall policy for the region'. These are *our lives* they are talking about." She sat up very straight at the table, her eyes bright. "And if we don't get anywhere through negotiating with them, then we're going to have to go for direct action," she went on.

"What's direct action?"

"Doing things to make people give you what you want," said Zillah. "I've read about it."

Zillah has read about *everything.* "What sort of things?" I asked.

"Blocking roads," said Zillah. "Guerrilla action."

"*Gorilla* action?"

Zillah rolled her eyes. "*No, Katie,* it's got nothing to do with gorillas. It means secret warfare. Thing is, we're local. We know the territory. We come out of the jungle and we disappear back into the jungle."

"Or the brambles," I said thoughtfully. It sounded uncomfortable. But Mrs T's eyes were sparkling.

"You've got it, Zillah. Richard can't get involved, because he's the head teacher. But I can, and I most certainly *will*."

Zillah and I looked at each other again. We didn't have to say anything. We knew for sure that we would, too.

Direct action.

"Perhaps we all could go on strike," I suggested.

Zillah frowned. "No, it's got to be something no one's ever done before. Something that gets the newspapers here – maybe even the TV cameras."

"Nothing violent," said Mrs T. "No damage to people or property."

"All right," said Zillah, looking disappointed. "But that means I can't carry out my plan of kidnapping the Chair of the Education Committee and holding him captive in the chicken-house until he agrees to change his mind."

"Zillah!"

"Only joking."

Chapter Fifteen

Zillah slept over at my house. Mum told us that Janice was upset, and it would be better if she and Geoff had some time on their own.

After we'd gone to bed, I told Zillah about how Granny Carne had rescued me from Shift & Partner.

"Granny Carne said that man's mother wanted him to be a lawyer? But how did she –"

"I know. He looked awful. He went completely white." I shivered, remembering it.

"Perhaps she knew him," went on Zillah doubtfully.

"I don't think she did. I think she was just – you know, like telling his fortune. Only it was the past, not the future."

"She only does that when people want her to. When they come up to her cottage."

But I knew that Ludo definitely hadn't wanted Granny Carne to tell him anything.

"Maybe she knows *everything*," went on Zillah. "So that when she looks at us it's like looking through a window. She can see right inside."

I didn't like that idea at all. There are some things about me which I don't want *anyone* to know, not even my best friends.

"Let's think about direct action," I said quickly. "We could make a list."

List of possible actions

1) Have a protest march. (Where to? There's no one to see it around here, except people who already agree that the school shouldn't be closed, plus cows, sheep and seagulls.)

2) Protest march up in Truro? (Too expensive to get there. No one in Truro will care about our school anyway.)

3) A massive SOS demonstration, with posters and banners, on the road to St Ives, so all the visitors see it. ("They'll only gawp. They'll think it's the kind of thing we do down here all the time, for the tourists. They won't do anything to help," said Zillah.)

4) Didn't someone from round here once sail a boat all the way from St Ives to London, with a petition? ("What, you reckon we could do it in *Wayfarer*, do you, Katie?" said Zillah scornfully. "We'd sink.")

I stopped writing. It was true that Zillah's little boat *Wayfarer* didn't look as if it could sail all the way to London – or even Plymouth.

"OK," I said. "You have the ideas then."

"Something exciting, so everyone wants to join in. And something that makes good pictures, so that we get on TV."

"All right, what?"

"I don't know."

"Zillah! !!!!!!!!!******!!!!!!!!! You criticized all my ideas, and you haven't got a single one yourself."

"I'm too tired," said Zillah. "There's nothing in my head. And I keep thinking about Mum."

"She'll be all right."

"Yeah … but Katie, why did they fall for it?"

"It was like your dad said. They wanted to."

"They're such a responsibility," said Zillah. "I never know what they'll do next."

"You could ask Granny Carne."

"Thanks loads, Katie."

Chapter Sixteen

But it wasn't Zillah or me who thought of the idea. It was Susie Buryan.

Yes, Susie Buryan, the most boring girl in our school, Susie who thinks that a Guides Pot-Luck Supper is a thrilling night out, Susie who does her homework on time and never gets into trouble, who always has perfect sandwiches for her packed lunch and doesn't want her ears pierced in case they get infected, who helps her mother with the housework every Saturday morning, not because she won't get any pocket money otherwise but *because she likes it*. Susie strongly disapproves of Zillah. And of me, now, too, because I'm Zillah's friend. When I first came to Cornwall, Susie thought I might be her friend, and so did I until I found out what she was really like. Being Susie's friend would be hard work as well as boring, because you have to listen to her all the time and say "Yes" in all the right places.

So when Susie first had her idea, no one really listened. We were gathered round the chestnut-tree stump at lunch-time, while the little ones played hopscotch. There was Mark, and Bryony, and Jenny Pendour, and Zillah and me. And Susie was there too. Everyone was trying to think of ideas for direct action, but not coming up with anything.

"It ought to be based at the school," said Mark. "That way we'll get a photo of it in the papers, with all of us."

"But it's got to be something different – something we don't normally do at school, so that it'll get attention –" went on Bryony.

Everyone started suggesting loads of things we don't normally do at school.

"We could hack into the Education Department computer. Delete all their plans."

"We could do a play about them trying to shut the school."

"Yeah, and maybe someone really famous would see it and make a film and then –"

"My dad's got a shotgun."

"So what? So's everyone's."

"We could build barricades."

"Let's e-mail Yakutsk and ask for help."

"Let's e-mail the Prime Minister."

"Yeah... What's his name?"

Everyone was mucking about, getting rid of the tension that had been building up since Mr Trevelyan first told us the news about the school closing. By this time Susie had already said her idea twice, but no one had heard it. The third time, though, her words sliced into a moment of silence.

"We don't usually sleep at school," she said.

"So? What's that got to do with saving the school?"

Susie went on doggedly. "Well, we don't, do we? It'd be something different."

"What, sleep here at night, you mean?"

"All of us?"

"In our pyjamas and dressing-gowns?"

"I don't wear pyjamas, I wear a nightie."

"We could bring our duvets."

"No, sleeping-bags'd be better."

"And those camping mats. The floors in school are really hard."

"We'll have to put all the tables in our classroom against the walls."

"No, let's sleep in the hall, there's more room."

"But what are we doing it for?" asked Jenny Pendour.

"It's like –"

"We're not going to go –"

"You can't make us."

"We'll even sleep here."

"We'll stay here day and night."

"Until you change your minds."

"We won't go."

"We'll need loads of food."

"Yeah! Midnight feasts."

"We can put SOS posters all round the walls, then they'll be in the photos."

"Who's going to take the photos?"

"We are. And my dad's got a camcorder."

"We'll phone up the newspapers and tell them to come."

"And TV companies."

"How do you phone TV companies?"

"We can find out. I'll look on the internet."

"But if Mr T knows, he'll have to stop us."

"We won't tell anyone. Not even our families. We'll get it all organized first."

"What about the little ones?"

"They'll start crying and want to go home."

"OK, everybody over eight, then. Not the little ones."

"The mums and dads can bring the little ones, once we get started."

"But lots of us go home on the school bus. It's four miles to my house. How are we going to get back to school again?"

"And the school will be locked up."

"We won't *have* to come back. We won't go home at all. We'll just stay here. We'll refuse to leave after school. We'll spread out our sleeping-bags and get changed in the cloakrooms."

"Mr T will stop us."

"No, he won't. We'll tell him it's like – like a children's strike. He can't take direct action, because he's the head teacher. But we can."

"What *is* direct action?"

"Doing things to make people give you what you want. That's right, isn't it, Zillah?"

"That's right."

"Jenny, you've got a mobile. You'll have to call our parents and tell them what's going on."

"We'll phone them once it's all set up. Then they can't stop us."

"They might not even *want* to stop us. None of our mums and dads want our school to close, do they?"

"How many over-eights are there in the school?"

"There are twenty-nine in Key Stage One. So it's all the rest of us."

"Sixty-eight take away twenty-nine – that's forty-one."

"No, it isn't, Jenny, it's thirty-nine."

"It'll be a real strike."

"It'll be a sit-in."

"No, a sleep-in!"

"Hey, Susie," said Mark, suddenly remembering who'd thought of it. "It's a good idea."

Susie flushed, and tossed her curls in the irritating way she does when people pay attention to her.

But the expression on her face was new. Susie was going to be bad for once. She was going to have a good time.

Chapter Seventeen

It's so hard keeping everything secret from Mum. When you're thinking about a plan all the time, the wrong words easily slip out. We've got phone numbers and e-mail addresses for all the local papers and TV companies. We've even got some national numbers, just in case. I've smuggled loads of Mum's posters into school, and hidden them behind the cleaners' cupboard.

Mark's organizing the food, because he and Bryony can get a lift into school if they tell their mum they've got to take loads of equipment for our environmental walk. We had a collection and got thirty pounds for food and drink, and Mark and Bry are going to buy it. We reckon we'd better not try to cook, or they'll say it's a fire-risk and that'll be an excuse to get us out of the building. Mark and Bry are buying biscuits and crisps and apples and chocolate and loads of drinks, and everyone's going to bring extra food in their lunchboxes as well. We keep remembering more things we're going to need. Torches. Towels. Toothpaste.

We have told so many lies. Here are some of them:

Lies to our parents
1) We need to take our sleeping-bags into school because we're doing a project on insulation in science and Mr T wants us to test our bags.

2) Mr T also wants to test the insulation and resilience of camping mats. However, there is no risk of damage to any equipment brought into the school.

Lies to our teachers
1) Robbie Sale has told Mr T that loads of us are having a sleepover at his mum and dad's caravan park. In tents, of course. This is the reason for all the sleeping-bags and backpacks coming into school. Luckily Mr T is more likely to believe this than Mrs Isaacs. She's much less vague than he is. She might even phone the Sales to check. Mr T, however, is just glad we're going to have a good time.

2) We've told Mr T that the sleepover's on Friday, because even he wouldn't believe that any parent would organize a sleepover in the middle of a school week. But we've also told him that we have to bring our sleeping bags and camping mats into school on Wednesday, because Mrs Sale is collecting them

119

after school. We all keep talking loudly about how we can't wait for Robbie's sleepover. (Wednesday is the day of action. Friday night is no good, because we think that all the local TV and newspaper reporters will be in the pub on Friday night, instead of in their offices to take our calls.)

There are more lies there than I've counted. You see how one lie leads to another? It all gets *very complicated*. But we can't help it. Once you start, you've got to keep on.

The biggest lie of all is that we aren't planning anything to help save the school. We watch Mr T trying to look cheerful, and Mrs T yelling at the little Ts because she's upset, Mrs Isaacs pretending that she doesn't mind retiring early, and all our mums and dads rushing about with petitions and letters and posters, and we keep quiet and don't say a word in case anyone guesses. I overheard Mr T talking to Mrs Isaacs in the hall when I was going out to the toilets.

"The children have taken it quite well, haven't they? They don't seem too upset."

"It won't become real to them until it actually happens," said Mrs Isaacs, rather sadly.

I'm holding my breath. We're all holding our breath. Only two days until Wednesday.

I wish I could see into the future now. I wish I knew if our plan was going to work. Will there be TV lights shining on us, and reporters scribbling in notebooks, and all of us in the classrooms at mid-night telling them that the school isn't going to close because we'll stay here until they change their minds? Or will it all fall apart? Will we give in when the first adult gets angry with us and yells at us to stop all this nonsense and get off home because we're keeping the school bus waiting?

Zillah won't give in. I know that for sure. And I don't think Mark will, or Bryony. Jenny ... I don't know. Jenny cries quite easily, and she hates argu-ments. It's difficult to guess about Susie. Robbie's pretty tough...

But what about you, Katie?

I don't know. Scared again, I know that.

Scared, aghast, apprehensive, terrified, fearful, nervous, paranoid, disconcerted, afraid.

But excited, too.

Chapter Eighteen

The long finger of the classroom clock dragged its way downwards. Quarter-past three. Twenty past. Twenty-three minutes past. The big hand shuddered, just a little, each time it clicked off another minute.

Almost time. The classroom crackled with the static of our built-up waiting. I glanced at Zillah. She was pretending to read, but she was watching the clock, too.

"Zill!" I whispered. "Two minutes to go."

"Yeah."

The second hand swept round. Everyone was looking at it now, except Mr T. He was deep in his computer, printing out e-mail from a school in North Carolina which had asked us for help with family history research. As usual, he hadn't noticed that it was nearly home-time.

"Sir, sir! It's time to ring the bell."

At the word "bell" Mr T leaped up. Our school bell sits on the top shelf by the classroom door. It has been our school bell since the beginning of time. It's very heavy and it's made of brass with worn-away writing around the edge. Zillah's dad says his dad told him it was Latin writing. There's a wooden handle that hundreds of hands have polished. We have a rota for ringing it, but we usually let Mr T do it, because he enjoys it so much. He seized the bell, opened our classroom door and began to ring it so vigorously that not only the little ones in Mrs Isaacs' class, but his own children in the house next door, could easily hear it.

Half-past three. No one moved. Mr T didn't notice it at first, because he was so happy clanging the bell. But at last he realized that something was different from usual, and he put down the bell and stared at us in a puzzled way.

"Er – I've rung the bell."

We were silent.

"You can go."

Slowly, we stood up. We could hear the little ones running across the hall. Some of them are met in the playground by their parents, others go home on the school bus. We wanted them out of the way before we began our action. Very slowly, we got stuff out of our drawers and put it into our backpacks. Very, very slowly, we fastened up our backpacks, put our chairs on top of our tables, asked each other questions about homework, had drinks of water at the sink, and looked for our lunch-boxes.

"You'll miss the bus if you're not careful," said Mr T crossly. "I can't hang round here waiting for you lot, I've got a pile of paperwork this high waiting in my office. I'll be back here in FIVE MINUTES and I don't want to find ANYONE still in the classroom."

He went out. At lightning speed, we grabbed our sleeping-bags and camping mats from the library corner where Mr T had let us stack them. Someone giggled.

"Shut *up*. We've got to get these into the hall before they hear us."

We were in the hall. We split up into our previously-arranged groups, and began to set up camp. Unroll the mats, spread them out. Lay out sleeping-bags on top. Mrs Isaacs would be out at the school bus, seeing the little ones into their seat with the parent volunteer.

Mr T's office door was shut. No time to change into our nightclothes – we'd do that later. Each of us unzipped our sleeping-bag, wriggled in, lay down and zipped the bag up tight. It felt so weird to be snuggling down in the school hall, which smelled as usual of polish, school dinners and old daps.

Two sleeping-bags were empty. Robbie was in the classroom, e-mailing like crazy. Bryony was outside, round the back of the school building, phoning a list of numbers on Jenny's mobile.

Footsteps. The door to the playground banged. It would be Mrs Isaacs, coming back in, along the corridor, into the hall –

Silence. I peeped out of my bag. She was standing dead still, her hand on the doorknob, staring. Then she called, "Mr *Trevelyan!*"

Of course. Her first thought would be that we were taking part in some weird Mr T project, and that he'd forgotten to tell her about it.

Mr T's office door opened immediately. (Mr T is quite afraid of Mrs Isaacs when she shouts.)

"Mr Trevelyan, please tell me what is going on. Aren't some of these children supposed to be on the school bus?"

Mr T came out of his office. He gaped at the hall floor, the camping mats, and the sleeping-bags with his class curled up inside them.

"But – but Mrs Isaacs, I don't know anything about this –"

Mark climbed out of his sleeping-bag, and stood up, facing them. We'd planned it all. *Don't wait till they start shouting. We've got to get in first.*

"We're taking direct action, sir. We've organized a sleep-in for tonight, in protest against the plan to close the school."

Mr T and Mrs Isaacs looked at each other. A kind

of light came over Mr T's tired, stressed face, but he said nothing. Mrs Isaacs cleared her throat, and said in the firm, friendly voice that always works when one of the little ones starts being silly, "Well, you've certainly made your point. But we don't want you to miss the school bus, do we? Your parents will be worried."

"No, they won't," said Mark. "They know what's going on. And we've already contacted the media."

"*Contacted the media!*" repeated Mr T. He ran his hands through his hair until it stuck out on end. Mrs Isaacs looked round sharply, as if she expected to see a TV reporter in one of the sleeping-bags. And then I heard a very familiar sound. The yelling of an angry baby, coming closer and closer. Footsteps hurried down the corridor, and there was Mrs T, with the two little Ts clinging to her legs and the baby in her arms –

"Richard, the bus is waiting – driver's furious, he's been banging on our door – woke the baby up – where are all the chil –?" She saw us.

"It's a protest against the school closure," said Mr T. "They've organized a sleep-in."

Mrs T stared at us. I could almost see her thoughts clicking. Slowly, a wide, wicked grin spread over her face.

"Wonderful," she said. "Just *think* of the publicity."

"Yes, just think of it," said Mrs Isaacs.

*　*　*

We had plenty of time to change into our pyjamas and nighties, dressing-gowns and slippers. We stuck our posters on the walls with Blu-tack, and got our home-made signs into position. Mrs T made Mr T and Mrs Isaacs go into the office.

"It mustn't look as if you've organized it."

"But we didn't," said Mr T. "*They* organized *us*."

And then we waited. Were they going to come? Had they believed us? Was it a big enough story?

It was. Regional TV just sent a reporter at first, but then she phoned for a camera-crew.

"The pictures will be fantastic – kids all in their dressing-gowns – teddy-bears on the sleeping-bags – fabulous old school buildings –" we heard her shouting into her mobile. Cars started arriving, one at a time at first, then more and more of them. There were parents, people from the local papers, radio reporters, TV people. Reporters kept leaning down over our sleeping-bags, and sticking big fluffy microphones under our noses.

"Right, now tell us, in your own words –"

"What's your name? Katie? Katie, how do you feel about this plan to close your school?"

"Did your teachers help you organize this?"

"What's your teddy bear's name?"

"Who's your leader?"

"What message have you got for the Education Department?"

"Look this way, all of you! Hold those teddy bears up! Now *smile.*"

We held up our teddy bears, because that was what they wanted. (The teddy bears were Jenny's idea. We borrowed them from people's little brothers and sisters, because of course we don't really have teddy bears any more, except perhaps for decoration...) But we also held up the signs we'd made. "Save Our School!" "We Want to Stay Together!" "Don't Split Up Our School Family." We were determined to get them on camera.

They interviewed Mr T and Mrs Isaacs too, in the office. Mr T e-mailed his statement to us from the office computer:

```
This is an independent action by the
children. I am remaining on school
premises with other teaching staff to
ensure the children's safety and well-
being.
```

More and more cars kept arriving, as well as people on foot. It was way past home-time, but the school was humming.

Mums and dads and grannies and grandads arrived from outlying farms. People were streaming in from the village, because they'd heard that something was going on up at the school. Each person who came immediately phoned someone else on their mobile. You know how it is when you light sparklers on bonfire night? It takes ages to get the first one lit, but as soon as it starts to fizz everyone else puts the tips of their sparklers close to it and they all burst into life at once? That's what it was like. Voices and people and the noise of car engines and mobiles making every kind of ring mobiles can make, and so many e-mails flooding into the computer that Robbie couldn't keep up with reading them. Robbie had e-mailed our Action Statement to everyone on our address list, and everyone was replying. He rushed back and forward from the computer in the classroom to the hall, reading out the messages to us.

"We're with you!"

"Keep it real."

"No to the closure!"

"Support the West Penwith thirty-nine!"

"Strongest greetings from your friends in Yakutsk!" (That's the school in Siberia we're linked to – Mr T says he's going to go there one day, when the little Ts are older.)

Mum arrived, with Geoff and Janice. Mum immediately sat down on a pile of gym mats with her sketch-pad, and began to draw the hall.

Janice cut up a giant fruit-cake which she'd brought. She laid all the cake slices on a white plate, so that they overlapped like flower petals, and then she came round and gave us one each. It was fantastic cake, sweet and moist and tasting of sherry.

"That'll keep you going a bit," said Janice.

Geoff walked slowly around the hall, reading the signs and the posters, his face grim.

"Is he angry with us?" I whispered to Zillah.

"He's all right. Dad always looks like that when he's reading."

Even the vicar came, and ate a piece of Janice's cake.

The two little Ts were having a great time crawling into sleeping-bags. The baby had disappeared, but someone said he was asleep on Mr T's lap, in the office. Mrs T was still making millions of phone calls, on her own mobile now, not Jenny's, because Jenny's credit had run out. Mrs T's posh voice had a brilliant effect. Everyone believed her straight away, when it had taken Bryony ages to convince media people she wasn't making up the whole story. (It is so weird, the way people never think that what you say is real, when you're young.)

It was late by the time the people from the Education Department arrived, with a man and a woman whom Mrs T said were local councillors. They were dressed in suits (Do they wear their suits all evening, then, as well as at work, or had they put them back on specially?) and they didn't say much.

They just muttered to each other and looked at everything. They wouldn't talk to the reporters either, they just kept saying *no comment.* All the parents surged around them, pressing petitions into their hands and holding up posters so they had to look at them. At first they wouldn't take the copies of our petition, or our Action Statement, but one of the dads shouted, "What've you lot come here for then, if you don't want to know what we got to say? You'll be hearing plenty from us next election if you don't listen now!"

All this time we stayed in our sleeping-bags. We'd been interviewed in our sleeping-bags, we'd watched everything from our sleeping-bags. *As long as you stay lying down, they won't be able to move you out.*

Mark leaned over. "They're all here now. Let's go!"

The whisper ran from sleeping-bag to sleeping-bag. "Let's go! Let's go!"

We all stood up. We each gripped a sign, and linked arms. We began the chant.

"*What do we want? To SAVE OUR SCHOOL.*
When do we want it? NOW!"

At first it was just us, then the parents joined in, then the people from the village. Everyone began to clap and stamp in rhythm to the words:

"*What do we want? To SAVE OUR SCHOOL!*
When do we want it? NOW!"

I could even hear the vicar's voice, loud and churchy, chanting along with the rest of us. And there was our community policeman, looking quite relaxed now that he'd decided there hadn't been a breach of the peace. He didn't join in the chant, but he looked as if he'd like to.

After a while the chanting died down. The vicar cleared his throat. I thought he was going to make a speech, but before he could say anything Geoff stepped forward.

We couldn't believe it. Zillah's dad *never* says anything at parents' evenings. Janice has to do all the talking. Zillah says the sight of teachers brings back bad memories for her dad.

But there he was, standing in the middle of the hall, his fists clenched at his sides. The TV people were still filming.

"It's not just the kids," said Geoff. You could hear the effort in his voice, but that only made it sound more real. "It's all of us. We're all in this together. Take away the school and you kick the heart out of us."

That was all he said, but it was enough. People stamped their feet again and clapped and cheered and waved their posters. It felt as if we could do anything, and they would *have* to listen to us.

Chapter Nineteen

If you've ever been out at dawn, you'll know that it's a strange time. Mum and I left the van at the top of the lane, and walked slowly home. It was grey and ghostly, and mist was lying on the fields in ribbons. You couldn't see the sea, but you could hear the gulls, and the birds waking everywhere.

I'd be able to get a few hours' sleep before school started again. Mum had said she'd drive me there in the van, which is much quicker than going round all the farms in the school bus. The West Penwith Thirty-nine had agreed that we would all be back at school at nine o'clock, so that no one would be able to say that the protest had "disrupted our education".

One by one, as it grew dark and all the reporters left, people had begun to drift away from the school hall. By midnight there was only us, and our parents. Some people had fallen asleep, others talked in quiet voices. The computer screens still glowed. Mrs T had made up a bed for the little Ts in a corner of the hall, and they were curled together like kittens, fast asleep. She and Mum talked for a long time. I heard the murmur of their voices, but not the words. Everything kept fading away, as I sank into sleep.

But the hall floor was hard. I woke up, stiff and sore, just as the sky in the hall windows was changing from black to navy-blue. Mum was bending over my sleeping-bag.

"It's dawn. You've done the protest. Let's go home."

All over the hall, my friends were stumbling out of their sleeping-bags, stretching and yawning, staggering off to the school toilets, helping their parents roll up the camping mats, dropping crisp bags and drink cans into a black bin-liner. Everyone was very quiet. No chanting or excitement now. Just cool, quiet dawn, and Mr T with his school keys waiting to lock up after us, and Mrs T carrying her children one by one back to the schoolhouse.

And now we were walking down the lane. Mum carried her sketchbook and my rolled-up sleeping-bag and camping mat. I had my backpack. I stumbled on a loose stone.

"Are you all right, Katie?"

"I'm fine."

I was fine. There was the roof of our cottage, half-hidden by the granite hedge. That hedge has been here for hundreds and hundreds of years. Zillah says that the Bronze Age people rolled those granite boulders into place, and let the hedge grow around them to enclose their fields.

"Maybe you've got Bronze Age ancestors," I teased her.

"Maybe I have," she said quite seriously. "We've always lived here. Most likely it was my ancestors that made these fields."

The light is strange at dawn. Quite different from any other time. Maybe, if I shut my eyes then opened them quickly, I'd see them: Zillah's ancestors, quick and strong, rolling those granite boulders into place, enclosing the fields for the very first time.

"What're you thinking, Katie?" asked Mum.

"Oh, nothing ... only how long things have been here."

"We haven't been here that long. Less than a year. Katie –"

"What?"

"Do you want to stay?"

Mum didn't ask the question as if she already knew the answer, or had already decided what was going to happen.

"I heard from the people who are renting our London house yesterday," she went on. "They like it there. They'd like to buy it, if we wanted to sell. We wouldn't make much money on it, Katie, because it's nearly all mortgaged, but it would give us enough for a deposit on a cottage down here. If you wanted to stay."

"Do you?"

"That's not what comes first," said Mum.

I saw our London house in my mind. My bedroom, Jessie living around the corner, our power-shower, the ice-rink only a bus-ride away, the park, the burger bar down the road, and all the shops. My old school, where I'd been since I was four. And Dad. Dad had never been to Cornwall. All my memories of him were London memories.

But I wouldn't be going back to my old school, even if we went back to London. I'd be moving on to secondary.

And although it had been great when Jessie visited after Christmas, I didn't want to phone her all the time any more, or write letters every week. Jessie was still my best friend in London, but she'd stopped being an everyday friend.

There's no ice-rink here, no cinema, no shops, no cafés. You could look at the fields and think they were empty. But down there was the cove where Zillah kept *Wayfarer*, and the beach where we swam. The coastal path was hidden in mist, but I knew where it was, and where it went. Zillah and I walked all the way into St Ives on the coastal path once. We went round all the tourist shops, and ate our fish-and-chips on Smeaton's Pier, and got the open-top bus back home.

I knew who lived in all the farms now.

I'd been up and down the lane to the Treliskes' farm hundreds of times.

I thought about all the other things. Lying in Zillah's orchard, reading our magazines and eating Janice's cakes. The noise of the cows coming in for milking.

Zillah sleeping over at our cottage and me lighting a fire in my bedroom, and us talking till midnight. Camping out in my tent in the garden in summer. Mark and Bryony coming over. Robbie Sale visiting on his dad's tractor. Mrs T bringing the little Ts down for a swim. Picnics down by Wicca Pool, and watching the seals.

Was Dad in London now? Would I find him there, if I went back?

Mum and I took Dad's ashes out on to the Thames. We went in a boat with Dad's friend Mick. Mick faced the boat into the wind and we threw Dad's ashes out on to the water behind the boat. Dad loved the river. Some of the ashes were heavy, and they sank at once. Others spread out on to the water. It was a grey day and Dad's ashes were grey on the grey water. Soon I couldn't see them any more.

"That wasn't really Dad. It was only his ashes," said Mum, and she put her arm round me and we held each other tight. The boat rocked as Mick turned her back to shore.

"*Where is Dad, then, if that was just his ashes?*" I didn't ask the question aloud, but Mum said, as if she'd heard my thoughts, "He's still with us, Katie, wherever we are."

"You mean, like a ghost?" I was younger then. I wanted to be sure. I didn't like the idea of Dad floating about the house, but never talking or laughing or putting on his music or shouting at me.

"No, not like a ghost," said Mum. "I don't really believe in them, do you? I mean whatever it was that made us love him: that's still here."

So Dad isn't in London, any more than he's in Cornwall. *Whatever it was that made us love him.* Dozens of memories crowded into my mind, jostling and sparkling. Dad tearing my school report into confetti because my teacher had said my Key Stage One test results were "disappointing". Dad helping me to choose my horse on Grand National day, and the time I put five pounds on an outsider called Maggie's Secret (I chose the name because of Mum). And my horse came in at 33-1. I remember Dad folding the notes into my hands and telling me the money was all mine, I could do what I liked with it. (I bought bunk beds with it. I'd always wanted them, for when friends came for a sleepover. And I took Mum and Dad out to Sunday lunch. It was great when the bill came, and the waiter gave it to Dad, and Dad said, "No, my daughter's paying.")

I thought of Dad moaning that he had terrible flu when he only had a cold, and me bringing him whisky with hot water and sugar, and Dad cheering up and playing cards with me.

Suddenly I thought of what Zillah had said about time being like a rolled-up carpet. We could only see the bit of the pattern we were living in. Only Granny Carne could unroll it, and see how the present joined on to the bits that had passed and the bits that were to come. She said they were the same thing. All one pattern, each part of it flowing into the next.

"Come on, Katie. You've been standing there for ages," said Mum. "I shouldn't have asked you to decide now. You're too tired."

"I'm not too tired. I was just thinking... Could we buy the cottage?"

"I don't think so," said Mum. "You know what Geoff and Janice are like. The farm's everything to them. They want to keep hold of it and pass it on to the next generation."

"But the cottage belongs to Zillah. Her great-aunt left it to her."

"You might find," said Mum carefully, "that Zillah feels the same as her parents, when it comes to it. The Treliskes have been here a long time."

"For ever."

"Yes. They won't want any of the farm going out of the family for good. But I think they'd give us a long lease."

"Does that mean we could stay in the cottage?"

"I think we could. But only if it's what you really want, Katie."

"Yes, it's what I want," I said.

As soon as I said it, I knew it was true. Not half-true, or even ninety per cent true. It was true all the way through, like the words they print into seaside rock.

But Mum was still looking at me expectantly, and I realized I'd only answered her question inside my own head.

"Yes," I said aloud. "It's what I really want."

The mist was clearing to blue. It was going to be another hot day.

Chapter Twenty

It's a perfect summer day. Not a cloud in the sky, no worries, just the sun on my back and the sound of the sea.

But so much has changed.

In a week, Zillah and I will have left school for ever. Well, not quite for ever, unfortunately. We've got to go to secondary school in September, but that's a whole summer away. We don't need to think about that yet.

No more Mr T. No more chatting to Mrs T over the playground wall, and Mrs T slipping us a C-H-O-C-O-L-A-T-E B-I-S-C-U-I-T each when the little Ts aren't looking. No more hours designing the most brilliant primary school website in cyberspace. No more helping the little ones in Mrs Isaacs' class with their reading, or planting organic lettuces in the school garden, or chasing the hens when they escape over the wall.

But although it's all ending for us, it's beginning to look as if the school will still be here. Nobody at the Education Department will admit that our Direct Action has anything to do with this. *They* weren't influenced by all the newspaper photos, or the radio interviews, or the item on the regional TV news. *They* don't care about the hundreds of letters of support that poured into the school. No, they are completely impartial. The case of the school closure is being decided entirely on its own merits.

But, as it happens, a directive has arrived from central government. Mr T read us part of it in Assembly. "*The government recognizes the vital importance of local centres of educational excellence in creating thriving rural communities. Such schools are a resource and a tool not only for the children and their parents, but also for the community at large.*" Mr T translated for us, "It means that we were right all along. We need our school. As Mr Treliske said, take away the school, and you kick the heart out of us."

"So we needn't have had our sleep-in, after all," said Jenny Pendour as we went back to the class-room after Assembly. "The government was going to keep our school open anyway."

But I don't believe that. I think there *is* a pattern. One things flows into the next, just as Granny Carne said. If we hadn't taken our direct action, part of the pattern would have been missing. But of course you can't really guess what the present would be like, if the past had been different...

Even people telling you what the future is going to be doesn't really help. Granny Carne looked so sure when she said to Zillah, "The sea'll look after you," that day when we went to her cottage. I really believed that she was looking into the future. But it still doesn't make sense.

There's a caravan park up at the farm now. Janice and Geoff's dream has come true.

But it's a very little caravan park. Shift & Partner would turn away from it in disgust. There are six caravans and four tents in High Field. Geoff mowed the field, and hired a Portaloo. There aren't any showers, but the campers and caravanners can come up to the farm to have baths. Geoff says it reminds him of summers when his grandma used to rent out rooms to summer visitors. Janice says she likes the company, but we know that what she really likes is the way the visitors are crazy about her cakes and scones.

We did teas for the first time last Sunday. We cleared out the farm parlour. There were three tables, with four places at each. The Treliskes have loads of old broken furniture up in their attic. Zillah and I cleaned up a set of kitchen chairs, Geoff mended them and gave them a coat of paint, and Janice made some new gingham seat-covers. They don't match, but they look great, and it didn't cost much. The tablecloths are gingham too. Janice is borrowing the WI cups and saucers and plates for the time being.

I picked marigolds for the tables while Zillah wrote a sign for the farm gate, and another one to put up on the road so that passing cars would see it and stop.

No one came at first. It was nerve-racking, because Janice had made dozens of scones and three big cakes: chocolate layer, coffee and walnut and gingerbread with lemon icing. There was strawberry jam and clotted cream for the cream teas. What if we were forced to eat it all ourselves? We kept going out to the yard to see if anyone was coming, and Zillah went up to the road twice to adjust the sign so that it was more visible.

And then it started. A family of five came up from the campsite: a mum and dad, two huge boys and a granny. It was their first day and they'd just put their big tent up, and they wanted a treat. They all had cream teas, and even though they said they were full up they also ate three-quarters of the chocolate layer cake. Janice kept whacking huge slices on to their plates, and Zillah kept telling her to keep them smaller or they wouldn't make any profit. (Zillah is in charge of the accounts.) Two cars drew up, with a couple in each, and then a group of hikers asked if we could do cream teas for eight in the garden.

"Twenty pounds!" Zillah hissed. "Quick, Katie, help me get the kitchen bench."

Zillah and I whizzed round, carrying the bench, the garden table and any spare chairs we could find into the orchard. The hikers said it was "idyllic", and they didn't seem to mind about the hens around their ankles, pecking up scone crumbs. When they'd gone, we found a two-pound tip under one of the saucers.

It went on until six o'clock. We were so busy that there was no time for Zillah to worry about dropping things. In fact, the only accident came when a little boy threw his orange squash on the floor because he wanted Coke. Zillah and I were exhausted by the end of the afternoon. All the cake was gone, and there was only one scone left, which we shared while we counted up the money. There was seventy-eight pounds fifty altogether. Zillah got out her calculator.

"Thirty-two people came, so they spent about two pounds forty-five each."

"Did you count the tips?"

"No, they're separate. That's another six pounds forty – six pounds eighty – six pounds ninety-five. Nearly three pounds each."

Janice is going to pay us five pounds each for the afternoon, if we work from two until six. With the tips as well, we'll get about eight pounds.

Janice has also agreed that from now on she'll make a few extra scones, so that we can have a cream tea at the end.

"I could have sold those cakes three times over," said Janice happily.

But Zillah was tough. "Make sure you give them smaller slices next time," she said, adding up the figures.

Janice and Geoff are making money. It's not much, nothing like the thousands and thousands of pounds Shift & Partner promised them. Shift & Partner aren't here any more, or at least . . . we don't think they are. . .

Susie Buryan's mum saw two men in a long black car near the school the week before last. They were taking photographs. She asked them what they were doing, because she didn't like the look of them. They said they were surveying the site.

"It's not a site, it's a school," said Mrs Buryan.

"Suit yourself," said one of them. I'm sure it was Ludo. And he grinned like a Cheshire cat, Mrs Buryan told Susie.

But no one's seen them since then. Perhaps they've really gone away for good now. I hope so. Sometimes, when I'm walking down the lane, I think I hear their car. The engine growls, as if it's after me, but when I turn round there's nothing there.

Zillah and I are going swimming in a minute. If I roll over and squint against the light to the entrance of the cove, I can see two sleek black heads, bobbing and diving. The seals.

It's eight o'clock. I'm back at the cottage, in my room, curled up on my bed. I've got my duvet wrapped around me, but I still feel cold. I told Mum I was shivering because Zillah and I stayed in the water too long this afternoon.

"You've got to be more sensible, Katie, or I'll have to stop you swimming down there without me."

Mum's going to come up with some hot chocolate in a minute.

"And if that doesn't warm you up, I'll have to try a mustard bath."

"Oh no, Mum, not the mustard bath!"

But I quite like it really. Mum doesn't often fuss over me. And hot chocolate and mustard baths are good things to think about, instead of miles of empty water and my own voice shouting, more and more panicky, "*Zillah! Zillah!*"

Zillah and I were in the water. I was swimming on my back, sculling with my hands, staring up at the clear blue sky. The tide was high, covering the beach, but the water was calm and we're very careful. There was just a bit of swell.

"I'm going to dive again," said Zillah. "Tell me if I keep my feet together this time, Katie."

She hauled herself out of the water, on to a ledge, then out on to our diving rock. The water's deep there, at this stage of the tide, and so it's safe to dive. There are rocks underwater, but Zillah knows where they all are, and she's shown me. I can do a racing dive now, but Zillah can do plain dives as well. That's the dive where you spring up and go down vertically into the water. There should be a straight line from the tips of your fingers to your pointed feet, and your feet should be together. Zillah's feet are usually almost together, but not quite.

Zillah stood on the rock with her feet together, poised, her knees bent, ready to spring. Beneath her the swell gently rose and fell, as if the sea was breathing. I pushed my hair out of my eyes and trod water.

"Are you watching, Katie?"

"Yes! Go, Zillah, go!"

As I said "Go!" one of her feet slipped. But only a little. Zillah swayed, caught her balance, and sprang. But the spring was wrong. There wasn't enough power behind it, and she didn't dive out far enough, into the free water. She plunged downwards, her legs over her head, driving her inward to the rock.

"Zillah!"

She was under the water. I couldn't see her. I dived down, but my eyes streamed with salt water and I still couldn't see her. I came up gasping, but the sea was bare. No Zillah. I dived again, swimming for the base of the rock. I thought I saw her this time, a dark shape twisting in the water, but I swam into a column of bubbles.

"Zillah! Zillah!"

And then I saw them. They were shouldering her through the water. Two dark sleek shapes, close together, with a third shape between them, borne up by them. It was Zillah. They swam alongside me, and turned their wet black eyes to me. The whiskers of the nearest seal grazed my cheek.

Zillah wasn't dead. She wasn't even unconscious, although I thought she was at first because her eyes were shut.

"Zill!"

We were back in shallow water now, at the base of the cliff, where there's our little beach at low tide. The seals pushed Zillah inward, and I grabbed hold of her and held her upright. Before they swam away, they looked full at me with their dark, intelligent eyes, as if they wanted to be sure I'd understood the message they were delivering. And then they were gone, turning, cutting through the water, going down and away from us in a long seal-dive.

"Can you climb on to the rock?"

Zillah nodded, eyes still closed. "In a minute," she said. I held on to her, in case the sea took her again.

"Did you hit your head?"

"I don't know. I kept on going down. I kept thinking I would start to come up but I didn't."

"The seals must have seen you."

Zillah opened her eyes. "What seals?"

"The seals that ... you know. Rescued you."

"I was swimming," said Zillah. "I was all right. You didn't need to worry, Katie."

"Can you get up the cliff path?"

It's a rough, steep path. Usually it's fine, but I was frightened now. What if Zillah got dizzy? What if she fell?

But Zillah seemed to be all right again. We clambered up on to the ledge where we'd been sunbathing, and wrapped ourselves in our towels.

"Katie, you look awful. You're shivering."

"I was so scared when you didn't come up. I thought you'd hit your head on the rock."

Zillah frowned. "I don't think so. It doesn't hurt. Did I keep my feet together, Katie?"

"No. It was the worst dive you've ever done."

I couldn't believe that Zillah didn't know what had happened. It was almost as if she didn't want to know. But it had happened, I was sure of it. I'd been so close to the seals that I'd seen their nostrils close as they prepared to dive. I shaded my eyes and stared at the sea glittering in the entrance to the cove. Nothing.

"They've gone," I said.

"They'll be back. They're always round here," said Zillah. She was feeling her head carefully. "I didn't bang myself, Katie. Just got dizzy down there for a minute, that's all it was."

They must have come in so fast. The moment Zillah dived, they must have sensed that something was the matter. They knew straight away that Zillah was in danger.

Just as Granny Carne did. It flashed through me like electricity. Granny Carne rocking, listening to something we couldn't hear. She could hear the pattern unfolding. Maybe she had already heard the splash of Zillah's dive.

It wasn't, "*The sea'll look after you.*" It was, "*The seals'll look after you.*" And then Granny Carne said she had nothing more for Zillah. Zillah was disappointed. She'd grumbled to me later on that we'd wasted our time going to see Granny Carne. Zillah wanted Granny Carne to tell her whether the caravan park would happen or not.

But if you're trying to find out about your future, you have to know the right questions to ask.

Mum's here now, sitting on my bed. The hot chocolate's got marshmallows on top, and Mum has sprinkled cinnamon on it too. She's brought her book up, and she's reading it. Every so often she stops and looks at me, checking me. Even though I haven't told her anything, Mum knows that I'm not cold and shivery just because I stayed too long in the water.

"I've got my radar," Mum used to say when I asked her how she knew things I hadn't told her.

I put my empty mug down beside the bed. "Mum, suppose you could see into the future. Do you think you'd be able to change it, or would you just have to live it?"

"Of course you can change things. Otherwise what would be the point of being alive?" says Mum.

"Do you believe that people can really see into the future?"

Mum hesitates. She looks serious, and I wonder if she is thinking about Dad. Then she says, very firmly, "No."

"Why?"

"Just no."

"I do."

"All right then, tell me my fortune."

"Give me your hand." I stare at the lines on Mum's hand. There are quite a lot of them. "Mm. I see an unusually talented and hardworking child . . . looks like it's a girl. . ."

"It's obviously not born yet," says Mum.

"Quiet. I'm trying to concentrate. I see fame ... and fortune..."

"Do you see a cottage with an outside toilet?"

"No, there's a proper bathroom now ... with a power-shower – you must have become rich..."

"Or perhaps my talented and hardworking daughter built it for me."

"A long lifeline – but I can see no more. You do mine now."

Mum takes my hand.

"I see a manicure ... in the very near future..."

"Mum!"

I am nearly asleep by the time Mum gets up and begins to tiptoe out of the room. But she stops by the door, and says in the kind of low voice that wouldn't wake me if I was really sleeping:

"Katie."

"Mm."

"What really happened down at the cove today, with you and Zillah?"

It all flashes through my mind, the pattern of events dazzling back and forth as if it is still being woven. Zillah going down and down, a dark shape in the dark water. The seals, rising to the surface with Zillah between them. Zillah's dive, her feet poised, her foot slipping: *"Go, Zillah, go!"*

Zillah with her eyes shut and her hair spread out on the water.

Granny Carne rocking to and fro, to and fro. *"The seals, Zillah. The seals'll look after you."*

The pattern moves faster. Forward, backwards. I can see all of it. But where am I?

I am here, now, where I belong.

"What really happened, Katie?"

"Nothing, Mum."